A Fresh Gale

A FRESH GALE

A NOVEL BY

WILLIAM SANFORD

Court Street Press
Montgomery

Court Street Press
P.O. Box 1588
Montgomery, AL 36102

ISBN 1-55838-065-3

Printed in the United States of America

To my classmate, Jack Solomon, ever the Professor, who read the manuscript, then revisited, with me, "Composition and Rhetoric 101." Thanks, Jack.

To my editor, Ben Beard, Jr. — the Patient One — whose knowledge, diligent work ethic, and sharply honed "cutting shears" brought this book to life. Thanks, Ben.

To my beloved, Cornelia Kreis Sanford, whose critiques, not of me, but of my writings, are invaluable. Thanks, sweetheart.

To many others, especially Ruth Walker, Julie Fields Bettress, and Dee Sanford Kelley, be assured that your input did not go unheeded. Thanks, Ladies.

To all who may come to read *A Fresh Gale*. Thanks. I hope that the story triggers a few memories.

Preface

Orphaned by the perils of war, Barton Sandeau returns to the place of his ancestors in hopes of solving the mystery of his birth, which has clouded his life for most of his twenty-one years.

In his search for his real identity, he encounters bigotry, racism, intrigue, prejudice, deceit, hoodlums, murder, mystery.

With the help of his newfound love, he weathers them all.

The characters in this story are fictional. Many of the places are fictional. The events, however, or some of them, could possibly be true.

Prologue

Flossie took the black-edged telegram, held it near her robust chest, stared at Ebb, wiped a tear from her eye and quietly stated, "Go fetch him."

Ebb kissed her on the cheek, backed out of the kitchen onto the porch parallel to the alley, slowly descended the recently repaired steps, opened the lattice doors, propped them, went into the garage, got into the '39 sedan, backed her out, drove down the alley to 19th Street.

In all of ten minutes, he was at the YMCA.

"Hope that foul-mouth man is not on duty," he said to himself.

He was.

"Could you fetch Barton Sandeau for me?"

"Let me see if I can find the little bastard."

Ebb cringed. He hated that word.

Chapter 1

Prospect Ridge

"Historical Marker One Mile." That's what is etched on the freshly painted sign of wood hanging on a post of cedar. At the Historical Marker, he drove onto the slightly rutted earthen path, parked, got out, went to the Historical Marker, read the wording, glanced beyond to the tall pine trees, envisioned the stately, firmly implanted, description of her school.

His vision, prompted by the stories told to him by his family, removed the full grown trees and replaced them with a beautiful two story, wood shingle building, much in need of a good paint job.

The sign: ORION MALE AND FEMALE INSTITUTE a short distance in front of him, was ever present in his imagination. So it seemed.

He recalled Aunt Alva mumbling stories about Orion Institute in between her verses of "The Spanish Cavalier." Sometimes she mentioned the Male Institute. "I suppose she forgot that it was a male and female school."

Motionless, he stood in awe of the beautiful structure looming against the dark blue sky and mesmerized in his childhood memories structured from the tales told to him by his family, now, seemingly, transformed the old structure to its original condition.

All the tales were becoming real, and he recalled them one by one. Several moments passed before his trance conjured up a visit. He began a slow walk toward the building still blanketed by the blue cloudless sky hovering over a bright sun. He stepped lightly upon the elongated porch. It spanned the entire front of the building.

Gas lamps were still hoisted to the ceiling. It would take a ladder to reach the tie-downs, latched out of reach, half way up the columns that stand guard over the well-worn porch.

Walking the breadth of the porch, he craned his neck, and actually saw the woodshed. According to the tales, it served as a detention hall and, when needed, as a discipline area. He retraced his steps on the small porch and peeked down the other side and saw, for certain, the stables. In his memories, he put fine gentle horses in them.

Returning to the entrance, he paused a moment, juggled the latch which unhinged on the first effort as the balance of the door was so expertly crafted that it swung open, inward, without any help. He carefully looked inside just in case he was not welcome.

Assured that he was alone, he walked inside to a wooden lectern with a sign hanging above it, and words:

> All students must sign the ledger upon leaving or upon entering the building. Each entry must have the date and time affixed adjacent to the signature. Failure to follow this rule earns an automatic five-demerit penalty.

Attached to the sign, above the ledger, a note written in perfect Palmer-method handwriting reminded the reader that copies of these ledgers were kept in the Library.

Wandering through the first level of the building and peering through the widely opened doors of the class rooms, creating imaginary situations of students filling the few remaining desks, he glanced toward the end of the hall where a steep narrow staircase led to the second level.

He approached the stairs.

The first step seemed dangerously loose. "All I need is to have an accident. Nobody knows where I am, and perhaps no one will be visiting this old place, so I best get along."

Outside, he walked toward his car, turned around, glanced back toward the two-story, frame, wooden shingle building, its bell missing from the belfry.

He flinched his eyes into the bright sunshine, looked again, and there appeared the full grown forest of tall pines.

At least, if only in his memories, he had seen Orion Male and Female Institute, his second planned stop.

His first planned stop had been the Bureau of Vital Statistics where he procured two very important birth certificates.

> Baby boy — unnamed — date of birth 01-12-27
> Father — unknown —
> Mother — Alva Sandeau
> Place of birth — General Hospital, Jefferson

Retracing his steps to the Historical Marker, he paused, looked again at the first birth certificate, stared at the word "Unknown" by Father, shook his head in disbelief.

He read the second birth certificate.

> Baby boy — unnamed — date of birth 01-12-27
> Father — Mathew B. Sandeau
> Mother — Hester B. Sandeau

Place of birth — General Hospital — Jefferson

Once more, he looked beyond the Historical Marker to the imaginary building, pondered, "Could my real mother, or his, have been a student here?"

Beyond the Historical Marker, the trees stood majestically under the bright orange sunshine with a pale blue sky as a background.

He sensed that many young females had once called this beautiful place, "their school."

Returning to his car, he started the engine, flipped the toggle switch of his radio, turned the knob, located a station, adjusted the volume, drove onto the highway, accepted with patience, his destined position — a safe distance — behind a big truck.

It was a good thing that he had listened to Ebb and remained a safe distance because a fast moving vehicle, horn blaring, in the adjacent lane, came into view of his rearview mirror.

A body flew out of the passenger side of the fast moving car. It seemed to have landed on the side of the highway, possibly being hit by another car. He couldn't tell exactly as he was trying to keep his eyes on the truck in front of him.

He passed under a wrought iron arch with an overhead sign:

WELCOME TO DEER HILL

Near one of the yellow brick mounts another smaller sign.

WELCOME TO DEER HILL.
12,000 FRIENDLY PEOPLE
2 OR 3 OLD GROUCHES.

"Doesn't every town have its quota of old grouches?" he said aloud.

Under the wrought-iron sign, into the City, still a safe distance, he followed the truck into the parking lot of the Motor Court and Cafe in hopes of finding a good lunch. His milk and doughnut of the morning had long been gone.

He was hungry.

Inside the octagonal two story building, a waitress beckoned him to a stool at the counter. He accepted.

"What'll it be?"

"The vegetable plate, ice tea, and pecan pie." Returning the menu to the waitress, he glanced at a window with a shelf on the outside near the side entrance where customers, mostly black who were not allowed to come inside, would order and pick up their food.

He remembered Ebb's remark, "Maybe, someday all of that foolishness will change."

He was almost finished with his food when a black man came to the window shouting for Mr. Brady.

Out of the kitchen came a man wiping his hands on his already soiled white apron. His sparkling blue eyes seem to glow as they focused on the black man at the window. Although his eyes were glaring, appearing to be angry that he had been disturbed from this already busy rush hour, his voice was gentle as he walked to the window and asked, "What is it Buster?"

The black man whose name had been called Buster by the man who must be Mr. Brady, very nervously shouted, "Mrs. Tom done fell out de car."

Mr. Brady looked at the staring customers seated at the red checkered oil cloth covered tables who had heard Buster's announcement about "Mrs. Tom."

Mr. Brady opened the side door and spoke, "Buster, come in here."

Buster, a tall person with olive skin and blue eyes, took off his wide brim, crumpled, felt hat and held it with both hands at a position near his belt, and as he entered through the side door he repeated, "Mrs. Tom done fell out de car."

Buster, known to most of the people now standing and gathering near him, nodded as if to say, "I knows that I'm not supposed to be in here; but, Mr. Brady done told me to come in."

Barton did not stand. He continued eating and occasionally turned toward Buster so not to appear totally indifferent to the tragedy of "Mrs. Tom."

One of the customers announced, "There goes Tom Bradleton's Green Cadillac. Boy, is he in a hurry."

Another person remarked, "He must be taking her to the hospital."

Another person stated in a smug matter-of-fact manner, "He must be taking her to Community. He's had run ins with the other hospitals. They are tired of taking up needed space to dry her out."

One obese and haughty lady whined, "I suppose that Clarabelle got into her 'tea' early today, don't you guess Maudie?"

The lady who must be Maudie replied. "Ah, Heather, don't be so rough on sister."

Mr. Brady took Buster by the arm, led him away from the curious crowd and into the kitchen.

Barton finished his lunch, paid the clerk the fare of one dollar plus four cents tax, left a ten cent tip, left the building and went to his car.

Two policemen were looking around his car.

"Something wrong, sir?"

"This your car?" asked the elder policeman.

"Yes. Sir." Barton responded politely .

"Let me see your driver's license," the younger policeman said.

Barton took his driver's license from his wallet, handed it to the young policeman who copied it on a tablet adjacent to his already recorded tag number.

The elder policeman inquired. "Are you staying in Deer Hill?"

"Hope so. For a few days." Barton replied, then added, " I have not found a place yet. Do you have any suggestions?"

The elder policeman returned the driver's license as he said, "Deer Hill Inn. And tell them that Chief Halsum sent you." Then he smiled and remarked, "Maybe they'll spring for a cup of coffee. Oh. And just so you know, I may want to interview you later. It seems that someone thinks that you may have witnessed the accident of Mrs. Tom Bradleton."

"Yes, sir. How do I get to Deer Hill Inn?"

The younger policeman, now a bit milder in his tone, gave the directions, "Continue on Three Notch Street, turn left between the Empress Theater and the Methodist Church. When you cross the railroad, you will see the sign."

"Thank you, sir," Barton replied.

He eased into his car, started the engine, and was backing out when he noticed the small truck parked near one of the small cabins behind the Cafe.

Buster was scrubbing the bumper and the hood.

He drove out of the parking lot leaving the gathered crowd to their futile effort to get the facts.

In route, he spotted the Estencrest Service Station. The sign read: EZRA WATKINS, PROPRIETOR. He pulled in for gas.

The pumps at Ezra Watkins's sat outside an overhang which

could hold only one car at a time. All others had to park outside. Barton parked outside.

A tall bespeckled man with a name tag —Watkins — came out of the small store, asked, "How many gallons?"

"She should take about ten, sir."

Mr. Watkins began to move the pump handle to and fro, peering upward watching the gauges on the glass container mounted on top of the red pedestal. The gas filled to the eleven mark. Mr. Watkins stopped pumping, took the hose from the red pedestal, inserted it into the tank on Barton's car, flipped a lever, allowed the gas to flow until his tank appeared to be full.

While waiting, Barton walked to a sign nearby and read:

HOTEL WATKINS. ALTITUDE 650 FEET. PURE ARTESIAN WATER. QUIET AND RESTFUL. PRIVATE GARAGES, PUTTING GREEN. ALL MODERN CONVENIENCES.

On the post of the sign were two wooden arrows. One pointed South: Miami 781 Nautical Miles. The other arrow pointed North: Chicago 781 Nautical Miles.

"This spot is exactly halfway between Miami and Chicago." Barton grinned.

"That's what the sign said. This might be a nice place to stay; but, I don't want to deprive the Chief of a free cup of coffee."

He paid Mr. Watkins the $1.34 for the gas, got into his car, drove to the next intersection of US 29, US 231, Beeline Highway #7, and North Three Notch Street, all being one and the same route to downtown.

He turned right, drove until he came to the Empress Theater, turned left, drove about a block and saw the sign for the Deer Hill Inn.

CHAPTER 2

Anne Marie Marbling

Ann Marie Marbling, home from Randolph College for females, attending a Champagne Brunch in honor of Sylvia Elaine Castille—bride elect of one Joseph Brevard Tillman, and reputed heir-apparent to the much-discussed Tillman fortune—joined eighteen of the loveliest debutantes of Deer Hill. Most of them were home from their respective schools, and all were attendants in the much publicized society wedding.

But whether an attendant or not an attendant, all were home to celebrate the many parties given in honor of Sylvia Elaine Castille, only daughter of widow Charlene Castille and the late Franklin Oliver Castille. And, in her own right, the sole heir to a Cotton Brokerage business which her beloved mother, Mrs. Charlene, has a life estate.

And, in her own right, Sylvia Elaine Castille, although at the age of twenty-four and an attested virgin; which is one of the traditional requirements of a bride of a Tillman male, also carried a healthy air of sweetness and charm that won the approval of the groom's mother, Mrs. Adie Tillman.

Mrs. Adie, holding court with the mothers of the many debutantes, expressed pleasure about her son, now at age of thirty-two and about to be married.

Sylvia Elaine moved from the head table to see what all the

giggling was about at the table where Mary Louise was holding court with the many young ladies who were almost, if not totally, inebriated from the champagne.

As usual, when not in mixed company, when that many young ladies get together, they revealed to each other their experiences whether fictitious or real. The champagne, in all of its splendor, enhanced and elaborated these stories which, with few exceptions, were merely imaginary.

Mary Louise had just commented that she could not come close to qualifying as a wife of a Tillman. She held her hand across her heart to attest. She also knew that her revelations, plus the generous consumption of the champagne, and the beautiful seductive setting cast among fresh flowers of every description with aromas challenging the weakest of nostrils, were creating an excitement among her young audience.

One member of the audience, Ann Marie Marbling, listening intently, was among those whose excitement was beginning to build. Her biological urges began to stir in her a feeling heretofore unknown or else not recognized. But, now in this festive mood along with the many revelations that she heard, her body and mind began to experience a new and sensuous desire.

Mary Louise timidly told Ann Marie and the other girls that they would know when the time would come for an intimate encounter with their beau.

Ann Marie knew. Beau or no beau. She eased out of the almost-ended champagne luncheon and moved into the lobby, taking what she thought was an unnoticeable position near the broad marble stairway where she observed one handsome young man checking into the Deer Hill Inn.

Her quick wit and intelligence had already devised a plan for meeting this young man, so she wasted no time in approaching him and asking, "Are you in town for the big wedding?"

"No, ma'am! I'm in town to do some research on my family, and I may check out the college while I'm here."

He held out his hand to her and stated, "I'm Barton Sandeau, and I would like to meet some people while I am here."

Ann Marie fluttered her dark blue eyes and responded, "I'm Ann Marie Marbling, home from college, and attending the many engagement parties of Sylvia Elaine Castille."

She felt a very slight wooziness and again fluttered her dark blue eyes as she stroked her heavy eyebrows with her left unringed finger and continued, "And, I also attended a debutante ball where I danced most of the evening with my father and my uncles."

Barton listened with interest and realized that he was still holding her soft right hand in his. He smiled. Released the handshake and gently spoke, "I enjoy dancing, especially with pretty girls."

She poised herself after a slight burp. "Why don't you get settled in, then I will show you our town."

He replied, "Thanks. Can you give me about ten minutes?"

She nodded in the affirmative, and thought to herself, "I'm going to give him a lot more than ten minutes."

She already knew the room number that she noticed on the big key ring of the hotel. It was 214. But now, she had to get by Sylvester, the elevator operator.

Sylvester, in his late sixties, had been employed by the Deer Hill Inn since the turn of the century. He had come from the head dishwasher in the famous kitchen, to chief bell man and elevator operator. In his years of service, Sylvester had grown wise to the ways of men and women. And, he knew almost everyone in Deer Hill. Sylvester was a trusted soul of many and had made many friends.

Sylvester was about to make another friend: Ann Marie Marbling.

Looking at Ann Marie, he glanced at the wide marble staircase indicating "take the stairs." Then he spoke quietly, "Give me five minutes."

Her body was giving way to a slightly limp condition, but she had not yet thought much about it. "You have come this far," she told herself, "so don't back out now." Mary Louise had told her earlier, "You will know."

Sylvester had ridden the open, highly polished brass and mahogany elevator lift to the second floor, and he had with him, a chilled bottle of champagne majestically resting carefully in a large silver bucket. The cork and the linen napkins rested on the ornate silver tray which also held two delicate, finely decorated champagne glasses.

He stepped from the elevator in his bright red jacket with velvet lapels and bountiful brass buttons shining above well creased, black, neatly pleated trousers hanging just above his highly polished slippers. He paused a moment, put his white-gloved finger to his lips as if to say to Ann Marie, "Give me a second."

He tapped on the door of room 214.

The door opened and in it stood Barton Sandeau, still dressed in his blue blazer and khaki trousers. His red and black tie was loosened at the neck.

He looked inquisitively at Sylvester who gave him an accomplished smile and spoke, "Mr. Sandeau, our compliments to you."

Barton inquired, "Two glasses?"

Sylvester nodded his gray-haired head toward Ann Marie who was standing a very short distance down the hall.

Then he left.

CHAPTER 3

Treasured Moments

Barton, with a reassuring fixed gaze, looked into her dark blue eyes which now appeared to be a little flinching, yet still sparkling under heavy natural black eyebrows, and set in the most beautiful face that he had ever seen.

It was a slender face with a pretty nose which seemed perfectly fitted as it sat between those eyes protruded downward in a shapely manner as if guarding the pretty, wide, moist, red lips.

His gaze continued as he held out his hand which she took as she stepped into the room.

As she entered, Barton noticed her red blushing cheeks and the soft black hair which hung neatly and almost touching her well postured shoulders as he said, with a very gentle and soft voice, "I noticed you in the lobby before you spoke to me."

And, too, he noticed that her breathing was slightly heavy which caused her firmly encased breast to move gently up and down in a pulsating movement as if in the sway of a gentle breeze.

Remaining in control as his gaze returned to her most beautiful, almost tearful eyes, he said, once again in that reassuring, soft voice, "Welcome to my little corner of the world."

At this moment, Ann Marie Marbling, full of uncertainty, was not sure whether she was going to turn and run, or continue into the room, or break down and begin to cry.

She was feeling woozy from the champagne, and the strong, new, and pleasurable anxieties seemed to be in control of her body. With her long slender hand still joined to his, she continued further into the room.

As the door closed, she said to herself, "Pull yourself together young lady; you've come this far. So get on with it and find out for yourself."

With those thoughts, she removed her wide brim hat and carefully straightened the large pink bow which streamed down the back. Next came the pink, high heeled shoes. And after a slight not-sure hesitation, she began removing her beautiful white eyelet dress.

Down to her satin slip, bra, panties and sheer hose; her tall, slender, well endowed, tanned body was even more beautiful. Barton had watched the entire undressing ceremony with curiosity and with a great deal of interest.

He again reached out for her long slender hand with bright red nails.

She looked into his well-tanned face and his deep set, bright, brown eyes and extended her hand to him. For a moment, they both stood motionless, still gazing into each other's eyes. Then, with an 'I-trust-you' look, she moved into his arms and put her head on his firm shoulders.

His passions were ever so present, but he was still in control. He felt her warm body next to his and humbly whispered, "You know that you don't have to go through with this if you don't want to. You can leave or we can sit here and talk, or whatever."

Reassured by his gentleness, she moved her lips toward his ear and whispered.

"I'm a virgin."

CHAPTER 4

Lessons Learned

Holding this gorgeous lady in his arms and stroking her soft coiffure, Barton's thoughts drifted to Dr. Ragsdales's lectures on the ideal marriage.

Lectures on marriage, love or sex were not in the curriculum of any college especially Birmingham-Southern; however, many of the forward-thinking Professor—sponsors of fraternities, wisely, selected smokers wherein members could hear lectures, talk frankly, and learn about subjects seldom mentioned in households, or class rooms, or in mixed company.

The entire lecture series assisted young males in learning about the opposite sex, and helped them to attain a wholesome and respectful approach toward love and marriage.

He smiled as he reminisced about some of the remarks heard in the lecture series. "And, now," he thought, "here I am with a gorgeous specimen of a female, half undressed, asleep, and snoring. Any man in the world could cherish such a moment." He held her for a few more seconds, then quietly and carefully led her to the bed.

It was almost two hours later when Ann Marie awoke. Somewhat startled at her surroundings, she spied her dress lying over the chair. Her hat and bow were still there. And, almost afraid to check, she found her panties and hose still on her body. Her bra was unsnapped and her bountiful breasts were hanging outside her slip. She lifted them back into her bra and reached around and clasped it.

She smiled.

Her head ached a little.

She sat up, shifted to the side of the bed and looked around the room, spotting the silver tray with the champagne ensemble. Her mind began to reconstruct those events which brought her here. She noticed the note stuffed in the neck of the opened, untouched, bottle of champagne.

Slowly, very slowly, she made her way to the bottle and took out the note and smiled as she read.

> My dear virgin, hopefully your nap was sufficient to clear your dear and pretty head. Your snoring has a nice chant to it. Leave me your number and I will give you a call later on this afternoon.

He had signed the note with the shorthand script that his mother had taught him: "With all my love."

Ann Marie read it a second time, then held it close to her heart and decided then and there that she was going to marry this gentleman.

She dressed, made her way to the lobby, stopped to speak to Sylvester, left the Inn, got into her Mercedes and drove home.

Later that afternoon, Barton returned to his room and found a note lying on a pillow which was propped near the foot of the bed.

> My dearest of dearest who did not take advantage of my

situation, the phone no. is 1402. If someone else answers, tell
them that we know each other from college. Also, be careful
what you say. Our telephone operators have big ears.

She had signed it with the same shorthand script: "With all
my love."

He read the note a second time, then tried to visualize just
how beautiful she was. He put the note in his pocket and left the
room, descending the wide marble stairs into the lobby, making
his way to the bank of two telephones. He selected one and
replied to the operator, "1402 Please."

On the other end came a mature ladies' voice, "Hello . . .
o . . . o . . . oh."

Barton answered, "Hello, I'm Barton Sandeau, a friend of
Ann Marie's, may I speak with her, please?"

"Mr. Sandeau, this is Ann Marie's mother. She has run an
errand for me. But, she left word that if you called, I am to invite
you over to our house, and later you are to go to a cook-out that
the Castilles are having for Sylvia Elaine."

"That's very nice. How do I get to your house?"

He recorded the instructions and said good bye to Mrs.
Marbling, put the phone back into its cradle, pondered his
predicament for a second, then started back to his room. He
spotted Sylvester and gave him a big smile and a wave of thanks.

Sylvester grinned, returning the wave.

Barton climbed the marble stairs to his room, and was about to
enter when he heard noises coming from the adjacent room. He
ignored the noise and went into his room and began to tidy
himself. He brushed his teeth, combed his hair, brushed his
clothes, and checked his wallet for funds in case they were needed.

He opened his door, stepped into the hallway and there met,

coming from the room of the noise, a middle-aged lady and one of the shaggiest young males that he had ever seen. He politely spoke to them, rushed to the marble stairs and made his way down and into the lobby, waved to his newfound friend, and went to the curb where his car was parked.

He cranked the motor of his 1933 Plymouth, took another look at the instructions given to him by Mrs. Marbling, turned on the self-installed radio, rotated the knob until he got a loud signal of the local station, where some crooner was singing "On The Sunny Side Of The Street."

He listened to this tune which seemed to fit his very predicament as he drove his car onto North Three Notch, turned right, then a left on to a narrow street where he observed the many antebellum homes which surely stood guard over the heritage of this beautiful town.

Even the trees stood majestically in their orderly places with their limbs entwined forming archways of tunnels that covered the breadth of the cobblestone street.

Sun rays peeping through the openings shed a glow on the flowers, shrubbery, and neatly trimmed lawns. The entire stretch of the street was well manicured and offered a certain feeling of welcome to its visitors.

"What a beautiful place," Barton thought.

The Marbling house was not difficult to find. It was a two-story, old English Tudor-style house with ornate balconies protruding on three sides. The double front door with its oval-shaped, multicolored stained glass, reflected the afternoon sun, and presented a warm and inviting aura.

He parked his car at the curb, strolled the long sand stone walkway between the borders of recently trimmed Chinese privet shrubs.

He lifted the heavy metal knocker and gave two gentle knocks which brought Mrs. Marbling to the door. She held out her hand and greeted Barton, announcing that Ann Marie had not yet returned, but she should not be much longer.

Mrs. Marbling had just finished uttering her words when a car pulled into the drive. Out jumped Ann Marie, leaving the door ajar, rushed to Barton, took his face in both of her hands and planted a very decisive kiss upon his lips.

Mrs. Marbling, with eyebrows raised, and somewhat of an approving smile, said, "I see that you two know each other."

Ann Marie, still clutching his face, answered, "We sure do, Mama."

She released Barton's face and turned to her Mother and inquired, "Is Father home yet? I want him to meet Barton."

"I phoned him that Mr. Sandeau was coming over, and he plans to be here before you leave for the lodge. He did say something about Clarabelle Bradleton falling out of the car and that she was dead upon arrival at Central Hospital. He and the Coroner were going over to Tom Bradleton's to console him, and to see if there was anything that they could do."

She paused a moment then remarked, "I'm going to my bridge club." She patted Ann Marie on the shoulder and asked, "May I tell my club about your Barton?" She smiled at Barton and continued, "I get all of the news there, and sometimes we do get to finish our bridge game."

Ann Marie hugged her mother and proudly stated, "Yes, ma'am. You can tell them that Barton is the sweetest, most considerate man that I have ever met." Then she kissed her mother on the cheek.

Mrs. Marbling put her hand to her mouth and gave a very light cough as though she must be going, then she told them that the Judge should be home before they left for the lodge.

Mrs. Marbling had barely gotten out of the door before Ann Marie went to Barton and put her arms around his neck, planting a lingering kiss upon his lips. He put his arms around her waist, then moved them to her shoulders. The embrace lasted for several moments, and Ann Marie could feel the bulging in his pants. She knew that the time had come.

Barton withdrew from the embrace. "If we are going all the way, I need to go to my car and get something."

She smiled and responded, "Do you mean a condom?" And in the next breath stated, "By all means go to your car."

Within an hour, the Trojan three-pack was spent. Ann Marie was spent. Barton was spent.

They lay together with Barton's face between two beautiful, full breasts.

Ann Marie asked, "Did you undo my bra at the Inn?"

Barton answered, "Yes, but only to make you more comfortable. And, I did plant a small kiss right here." He kissed the deep valley between her breast and she began a pleasing quiver. When he moved his lips to her nipples, she led him to her. In no time he had entered her for the fourth time, and this time there was no protection.

CHAPTER 5

The Bridge Club

The Country Club was like a beehive. The parking lot was overflowing with cars from surrounding counties and in such quantities that Justin, the parking attendant, had to temporarily park them on the curb, on the lawn; but, certainly not on the almost sacred ground —the golf course.

Today was Thursday. The one Thursday in the month that the Bridge Club could invite guests. And this Thursday they invited the Castille-Tillman wedding entourage. That is, those who had rested from the Brunch.

With plentiful guests, and plentiful finger foods, and plentiful beverages, the crowd at the club that afternoon was most congenial.

Mrs. Marbling had left her car with Justin and entered the foyer where she was met by Mrs. Paul Bydian who eagerly remarked, "Ellen Langur tells us that Ann Marie has a house guest."

"News does travel. I just met him, myself, a few moments ago, and I'm not sure about Ann Marie's plans." She winked at Mrs. Bydian and continued, "But he does meet with my approval."

Mrs. Paul Bydian laughed and suggested that they join the overflowing crowd in the ball room and visit with some of the

Castille-Tillman guests. She thought a moment and grinned, "We already know the guest of the Bridge Club."

They stopped to visit with Mrs. Flora Minsky who was seated in a high-back chair near the punch table and greeting people and using both hands to shake. She had Mrs. Bydian's hand in one of hers and she had Mrs. Marbling's hand in the other, telling a third person about poor Clarabelle Bradleton. Mrs. Minsky, at the age of 92, was still alert and could call most everyone by their maiden name, particularly if they had been born in Deer Hill.

Mrs. Marbling and Mrs. Paul Bydian passed through Mrs. Minsky's self-appointed chamber near the punch table, and made their way among other guests. And, each time the fate of poor Tom Bradleton was being discussed, everyone seemed to be concerned. Yet, one was not. Widow Ellen Langur merely nodded her wrinkled old face, empty of compassion. She always acted superior, as if she were privy to information others were not.

When the gossip shifted to the Castille-Tillman wedding, and the lovely girls who were to be the bridesmaids, most of the many conversations ceased in favor of the fine finger foods being served by the many waiters carrying silver trays.

And, these waiters knew how to cater to the ladies who held themselves out to be descendants of the founders of the Deer Hill.

Henri, the most notable of the waiters, had just bent to serve Mrs. Minsky, when the announcement came that all who wished to play bridge should submit their names to Mrs. Paul Bydian who was in charge of today's meeting.

No one seemed to budge.

After several futile attempts to organize the bridge, Mrs. Paul

Bydian, in consort with several others, announced that the bridge game has been canceled.

This pleased Mrs. Minsky, who could continue her reign in the high-back chair near the depleted punch bowl where she was congratulating Mrs. Tillman on the wedding of her son, Brevard, to Sylvia Elaine Castille.

Mrs. Tillman stated, "Flora, it's about time my dearest and eldest found a wife." And noticing Mrs. Castille who had moved nearby to pay her respects to Mrs. Minsky, she, in a quick afterthought, uttered, "And, he could look the world over and not find a young virgin lady more suitable to us than Sylvia Elaine."

The shy Mrs. Castille smiled approvingly. She thought about Maudie Jefferson's statement about the nice ladies who claimed to be descendants of the founding fathers, or else, in their terms, "have roots."

Mrs. Maudie Jefferson, not being among those accorded roots, often remarked, "There are two places where these old biddies are recognized: in Church, and at that damn club." She would smirk and add, "And, I doubt if any of them ever knew what a good root was."

Mrs. Castille dismissed her thoughts about Mrs. Maudie, and about the roots of the community, and turned to bid farewell to the many guests who were now leaving.

A few lingering guests were in court with Mrs. Minsky, and she was telling them that most of the old money of Deer Hill came from European Cotton Merchants such as her forefathers. But there was one family who brought gold from elsewhere, and that family was the Tillmans. And she added with an smirk of insolence, "And when we went off the gold standard in the thirties, they took their gold to Switzerland."

Her eyes gleamed as she told the stories about the money in Deer Hill, and she appeared to know just how each one came upon such wealth.

When it was time for Mrs. Minsky to leave, Justin helped her to her car which was driven by her chauffeur of thirty years.

All the guest had departed the club, and left lingering was Mrs. Paul Bydian, Mrs. Stanley Tillman, Mrs. Bolton Castille, and Mrs. Henry Marbling. These four ladies had something in common with many of the families of Deer Hill. Their families or the families of their husband's had come to Deer Hill as Cotton Merchants prior to the Civil War of 1860, and, to most people of Deer Hill, these four were acknowledged and were accepted as being keepers of the "roots." And one of the real reasons that they were so acknowledged was that they never ever mentioned it, nor did they put much emphasis on it. And as one newcomer had expressed it, "They move among the citizens without any air of superiority."

CHAPTER 6

The Lodge

Barton lingered in his warm bath with his thoughts on Ann Marie. Everything about her was beautiful; her laugh, her sensuousness, her responsiveness, and even her gleeful shout when her hymen separated. He thought, "I will always remember her whisper, 'now I'm a woman.'"

Not then, but now in his thoughts, he believed that Ann Marie had sought the moment, and the man for this event.

"I'm glad she chose me," he whispered aloud to himself, as he stepped out of the four-leg, cast-iron bath tub and began drying with the small bath towel provided by the hotel.

Dressed in gray slacks, a solid blue open-collar shirt, and a navy blue sweater, Barton descended the wide stairs to the lobby of the Inn. He glanced around looking for his newfound friend, Sylvester, but did not see him so he went outside to his car.

Two policemen were walking round his car as if they were looking for something. When they saw Barton, they got into their car and drove away.

To Barton, this was strange. This was the second time in one day that his car had been inspected by the policemen. He watched the policemen's car until it was out of sight then he got into his car drove over to Walnut Street, parked in front the gothic style Post Office building, got out and walked to Lanier's drugstore.

He entered the drugstore just as Sylvester was about to leave. He stopped momentarily and shook his hand. Several customers seem to be staring at him probably because he had shaken the hand of a black man. It did not matter to Barton; Sylvester was his friend.

He passed two distinguished looking men sitting on the stools at the counter, and thought that one them had spoken to him, so he turned and said, "Good afternoon, sir."

The eldest man smiled and replied, "And a good afternoon to you, young man."

Barton walked to the window at the rear of the store where a short, gray-headed man was standing. He was wearing a white cloak. Barton assumed that this gentle-looking man was the druggist.

"What can I do for you young man?" asked the Druggist.

Barton quietly and precisely replied, "One dozen Trojans, please."

The druggist took the package from the drawer and slid it to Barton. "That'll be three dollars."

Barton paid the three dollars, put the package in his pants pocket, and headed toward the door.

He passed the two distinguished-looking gentlemen, he spoke again.

One of the men turned slightly on his stool, smiled, replied, "And a good afternoon to you."

As he was entering his car a police car passed. The driver was the elderly policeman who had checked his license earlier at The Motor Inn and Cafe. The policeman put his arm out of the window and waved to him.

Barton returned the wave, got into his car and drove toward the natural tunnel of College Street with all of her entwined trees overhead, and her beautiful well-manicured shrubbery along the walkways and drives of the castle-like homes. Again, he whispered, "What a beautiful place."

He arrived at the Marbling home precisely at seven p.m. And was about to knock, when the door opened and Ann Marie with an accomplished grin and a low whisper, said, "Hello, lover." She then kissed him on the cheek.

Barton grinned, yet said nothing until he reached Mrs. Marbling. He shook her hand and asked, "How did your bridge game go?"

"It didn't. We had so many people that we were never able to do anything but listen to the gossip. How has your day gone?"

Before he could answer, Ann Marie announced that her father had phoned and that he would be late, and that her mother would be going with them to the cookout at the lodge.

Barton responded as he smiled, "That will be a pleasure."

Ann Marie spoke up, "We'll take my car, but you will have to drive."

"Oh no! We'll take your car, and you will drive!"

Mrs. Marbling laughed as she stood and took Barton's arm and said, "Mr. Sandeau, I think that I'm going to like you." Ann Marie smiled at both of them and agreed, "Okay, I'll drive."

The twenty-two minute drive to the lodge was a pleasure in Ann Marie's Mercedes. It was the first time that Barton had sat in a bucket seat in an automobile.

"This is a fine car."

"Thank you. It is a gift from my grandmother who lives in Oberammergau, Germany. She lived with us during the war, but went back to Germany as soon as she could. My uncles, mother's brothers, were involved with the German government, so grandma's property was taken care of by them." Then she ruefully added, "And she took care of their money which she brought with her to Deer Hill."

She paused a moment and continued, "Mama, is it true that the German boys held out at the prison camp were not exactly prisoners of war; but, were sons of wealthy Germans and were sent here to sit out the war in Europe?"

Mrs. Marbling responded, "I've heard that humor, and it is a fact that mother visited the camp often. She would make cookies for them. And, she occasionally wrote letters to the parents of some of them. We were very careful with her on that subject. She detested Hitler, but she loved her beloved Germany. And, she was instrumental in getting Mr. Moll der Vogh to take his high school band out there and perform for them."

All three were silent for a moment as if a great secret had been revealed. Then Ann Marie looked passionately at Barton and asked, "What are you thinking about?"

Barton solemnly replied, "Oh, I was just thinking about such an arrangement wherein wars separate people, yet, after each war the world seems closer to peace, and all people seem to get along for awhile until certain greedy groups want to control everything, like products essential to the economy of the whole world. Then it starts over again."

Mrs. Marbling spoke, "I remember my great grandparents who came to America as Cotton Merchants for the London and Liverpool Cotton Exchange and lived in Deer Hill from 1844 until 1860 when they were recalled to London because of the brewing of a civil war in the United States. Big papa, Jacob Klingenberg, often told us that the reason for the civil unrest in the United States was that European cotton buyers were paying higher prices for the cotton raised in the southern part of the United States." She let out a laughter and proceeded, "He often said that the Textile Barons took a page out of Napoleon's book. 'To create unrest. Then conquer.'

"And, that one thing, the price of cotton, antagonized the textile barons of the northern part of the United States that they actually hired journalists to write stories about slavery that would inflame the peoples of the world in hopes that the wrath would be so great that it would bring the southern planter to his knees and he would be only too happy to sell his cotton to them." She went on to tell them about her great uncle of the British Consular Service who claimed that there was documented evidence that cotton was actually the issue of the civil war, and that slavery was the catalyst for it. She quoted a heralded General of the Confederate Army: "If our troops believed that they were fighting to maintain slavery, then this war would not last ten days."

Ann Marie chimed, "I remember grandmother making a statement that the propagandists were not so much against slavery as they were against the southern planters."

Barton entered into the conversation and said, "If you recall, it is alleged that Mr. Lincoln stated that he wanted to preserve the Union whether it be all slave, part slave or no slave." He was silent for a few seconds, then added, "I am very much against slavery for anyone, in any form, even though the Bible has scriptures referring to slavery."

"Where in the Bible does it refer to slavery?" Ann Marie asked.

Without hesitation, Barton replied, "Twenty-first Chapter of Exodus, verses one through eleven, entitled Laws of Persons and Property."

"What is written in the twenty-first chapter of Exodus?" Ann Marie pointedly inquired.

Barton laughed as he answered, "I cannot quote it verbatim, but the theme seems to be that if a master buys a Hebrew servant, that servant shall serve for six years, and shall go out free in the seventh year. And, if the master has given him a wife, and then there are children, the slave may go out free, but the wife and children must stay as property of the master. However, if the slave sayeth that I love my master, I love my wife, and I love my children; I will not go out free . . ."

"Then what happens?" Interrupted Mrs. Marbling.

"Then the master shall bring him to the judges and there bore his ear through with an aul, and the servant shall serve the master forever."

"Barton, that is very interesting," spoke Mrs. Marbling. "Tell me a little about yourself."

Barton turned in the bucket seat so that he could see Mrs. Marbling and responded, "There is very little to tell. My grandparents farmed in Pike and Coffee counties, but abandoned the farm in favor of the railroad jobs. They moved from Pike County around 1926. However, they were returned here for burial next to my great grandparents in the Pleasant Hill Church Cemetery. Both of my parents are dead. My father was killed in Europe during World War II, and my mother, who was an airplane ferry pilot during World War II, was lost at sea somewhere near the island of Newfoundland."

Ann Marie winced. "How terrible."

Mrs. Marbling apologetically sighed, "I am so sorry."

He looked at Ann Marie then Mrs. Marbling. "Thank the both of you. I am at peace with that situation which has inspired many of my goals in life."

"Name some of those goals."

"Well, I would like to get a degree, maybe in History, so that I could teach if I chose. And, someday, I would like to get married to a beautiful girl, have a house full of children . . ."

Ann Marie retorted, "If I were your wife, we would have them four at a time."

Mrs. Marbling interrupted, "One at a time is enough."

Ann Marie was smiling as she drove through the gate and over the cattle walk and on to a circular, cinder-surfaced drive which led to the lodge. She parked the Mercedes on the grass. Barton got out and opened the door for Mrs. Marbling with a mock bow. Ann Marie came around and took Barton's left arm. Mrs. Marbling was holding his right arm. The three of them slowly walked toward the lodge and the already somewhat boisterous and lively guests.

Sylvia Elaine spotted the three with interlocking arms and ran the short distance to greet them. As she stopped to hug Mrs. Marbling, she turned her eyes toward Barton.

"Ann Marie, have you been holding out on me?"

"Certainly not. However, I do think that I will hide him from all those gorgeous young ladies gathered over there. Already, my mother has adopted him," she slyly answered.

Laughing, all four approached Mrs. Castille and Mrs. Tillman who were seated at a table where they greeted their guest.

Mrs. Marbling spoke to both of them, "Many thanks to both of you for including our guest, Mr. Sandeau." She then introduced Barton to everyone present. She smiled as his manners were perfect; the elder ladies seemed a wee bit haughty that their daughters were not as fortunate as Ann Marie.

After several introductions, Barton suggested to Ann Marie that they go over and visit with that young couple standing alone near the pool. She agreed and announced that she and Barton were going to mix and mingle.

Approaching the young couple, Barton stuck out his hand and said, "I'm Barton Sandeau, and this is my date, Ann Marie Marbling."

The young man smiled and appeared a little relieved to be talking with someone. He clasped Barton's hand and said, "I am DeNero van der Mueller, and this is my wife Maria."

Maria, a very beautiful, slender, dark-haired young lady with very strong features, and not much older than Ann Marie, spoke, "Mr. Sandeau, exactly how long have you been in Deer Hill?"

Barton smiled as he answered, "One day."

Maria and DeNero both responded with an askance look.

Barton, noticing their expression, politely explained that he had arrived in Deer Hill about noon, had a lucky break in meeting Ann Marie who invited him to the party. Then he added, "I did not mean to be curt, but I have been in Deer Hill only since noon today."

Ann Marie laughingly remarked as she shook hands with Maria, "And, he has covered a lot of territory in such a short time." Then she asked, "And, where are you two lovely people from?"

DeNero answered, "We are from Southampton, England, and we have been touring the United States on vacation. Brevard had written to us about his wedding, so we arranged to be in Deer Hill for this special event. We got in late this afternoon on the train from Jacksonville.

"Sylvester, at the Inn, met us, helped us get settled into our room, then drove us out here. Brevard left word that he would get us a ride back."

Ann Marie spoke, "Barton and I would love to give you two a ride back to the Inn."

DeNero replied, "Swell. Let me go tell Brevard so that he will have one less thing to worry about." Maria went with DeNero.

Ann Marie whispered to Barton, "Your date desires that you drive back to town. Your date desires other things of you later on in the evening. Your date herewith hands you the keys to the car. And most of all, your date believes that she loves you. And your date . . ."

She did not get to finish whatever else she was going to say because her mother and father were approaching at the same time that DeNero and Maria arrived back.

Before anyone could say anything, Judge Marbling shook hands with DeNero and Maria and introduced himself and his wife. He then turned to Barton and gave him a warm smile, and a very quizzical look as he shook his hand.

Barton returned the smile and said, "It is nice of your family to include me for this party."

The Judge replied, "Thank you. Ann Marie has told me that you golf, and we have so many guests for the wedding who want to play golf in the morning, and we need one more to round out the six foursomes. Can you join us at 9:30?"

Barton humbly replied, "It just so happens that I have my sticks in the car. Is it at the club or at the college?"

"The club." Then Judge Marbling thought to himself, "He is a very handsome young man, now where have I seen him before?" Before he could remember, his attention was attracted by the big dinner bell being rung. And, one of the servants announced that the food was ready.

Mrs. Castille stood and announced for everyone to bow their heads that Reverend Mulkin would say grace. Five minutes later,

Reverend Mulkin was still praising the event of a Christian marriage, and the good people who were participating, the good day that the Lord has made, and . . .

Mrs. Stanley Tillman, a major contributor to the church, fabricated a cough which apparently was a signal to Reverend Mulkin. He abruptly ended with an Amen.

Judge and Mrs. Marbling, DeNero, Maria, Ann Marie and Barton resumed their conversations with frequent pauses to greet or meet the other guests.

The line of people at the food table was quite lengthy, so Judge Marbling suggested that a few minutes wait would make the journey through the line more pleasant.

He had just uttered the suggestion and was glancing toward the lodge and the two people coming through the dogtrot. He turned to Mrs. Marbling and asked, "Is that not Jarvis Bydian coming out of the lodge?"

"I do believe it is, and he has that silly guitar with him." She took another glance in the direction of the dogtrot of the lodge and continued, "I have not seen him since he left town years ago when he got that farm girl pregnant and Miss High-and-Mighty, his mother, would not let him marry the poor girl." She began laughing and added, "The story goes that he was strumming that guitar and humming 'The Spanish Cavalier' when he got on the train headed out of town."

Ann Marie looked a little shocked that her mother would reveal such a thing. Then, she thought about this afternoon with Barton when there was no protection. She gave a shy and a somewhat rueful smile as she raised her eyebrows and looked at Barton.

He, too, had taken notice of Mrs. Marbling's words about the poor farm girl, and he guessed what Ann Marie's look was all about, and what she was probably thinking.

He moved to her, put his arm around her, and whispered in her ear; then, he moved a short distance to talk with DeNero.

Ann Marie seemed relieved and inquired of her mother why Mrs. Bydian wanted to send her son, Jarvis, out of town.

Judge Marbling spoke up. "She was afraid that the girl's family would do him harm. They were an honorable sort and were so embarrassed about the situation that they sold their farm and moved away."

"And he has not been back to see his mother in twenty years?"

"I'm sure that he has. I merely meant that I had not seen him in that long. I do know that his brother Paul, and his wife, visit with him in Florida."

Maria, who had hardly opened her mouth all evening, looked at Ann Marie and asked, "I wonder what happened to the baby?"

Judge Marbling, again responded, "A friend of mine, in Jefferson, who represented her family in a sanity hearing, told me that she gave birth to a baby boy and she never recovered from a deep-rooted depression. In time, her mother and her father had her committed to Brice's Hospital in Tuscaloosa."

Mrs. Marbling chimed, "Here comes Jarvis now, the old battle axe is with him. I notice that Paul and Betty are already in the food line. They had nothing to do with the mess, but they have certainly endured the wrath of Miss High-and-Mighty; and the gossip about it which nearly drove her insane."

The Old Mrs. Bydian, and Jarvis—with guitar—came over to Judge and Mrs. Marbling and exchanged greetings.

Mrs. Marbling introduced them to Maria and Ann Marie. She called to Barton and DeNero who were standing a short distance away but had not heard the conversation about the fate of the baby boy born to the farm girl.

When Barton turned around, he was only about three steps directly in front of the old Mrs. Bydian, who stared at him, took a deep gasp, dropped her cane, and fell fainted to the turf.

Dr. J.J. Beardy came over and examined her, then went to his car and got his bag.

The whole affair disrupted the party.

Judge Marbling told his wife, "I've lost my appetite."

"Me too, let's say our goodbyes and go home."

Ann Marie looked at Barton who said, "I'm ready whenever you are."

Ann Marie turned to Maria who said, "So are we."

The Castilles and the Tillmans seemed reconciled that the party was over because they stood waving and smiling at their departing guest as if to say 'the ole battle-ax' has done it again.

The Judge and Mrs. Marbling returned the wave as they departed for their car; but, Barton, DeNero, Ann Marie, and Maria hastily and without returning the wave, went to the Mercedes where DeNero opened the door for the girls to get into the back seat, then he crawled in beside Barton who had already cranked the engine.

DeNero rode up front at Ann Marie's suggestion so that she and Maria could talk. But there was no talk. Maria's head was nodding, so Ann Marie whispered, "Why don't you take a nap." And, in no time Maria was sound asleep.

The short twenty-minute ride to the Inn was very quiet as both Maria and DeNero were napping. When Barton parked the car in front of the Inn and opened his door, DeNero awoke and asked, "We here, already?"

Ann Marie tapped Maria on the shoulder and quietly spoke, "Wake up. We're here."

DeNero got out of the car and began stretching, then he

pushed the seat forward and helped his sleepy wife to the curb where he asked, "If you two don't mind, we are going up and get us a good night's rest. It's been a long day." He expressed gratitude to Barton and Ann Marie and walked with Maria through the large double doors.

Ann Marie looked at Barton and said, "Let's go into the Inn Lounge. I'll treat you to a night cap."

The Lounge was a small room completely encased in a rich mahogany wainscoting about one-third the height of the room, and the other two-thirds was covered with wall paper decorated in a foxhunt mural where the hunter's jackets were a very deep red, and the Foxes' fur was a deep brownish red. The hardwood dance floor was only about nine feet by nine feet, and adjacent to it, in one corner, was a piano.

Seating themselves near the piano, and speaking to the bartender at the same time, they ordered a Pabst Blue Ribbon and a frosted mug.

The Bartender asked, "Anything else?"

Ann Marie replied, "Do you have any food?"

"I think so. Let me check with the kitchen."

The bartender brought the cold beer and the frosted mugs and announced that baked ham sandwiches and potato salad was readily available.

Ann Marie wasted no time in answering, "We'll take two."

They sat in silence as they tasted the foam which had formed in their mugs. Ann Marie looked over the rim of her mug and began making eyes at Barton in a playful manner as if she wanted to tease.

Finally, Barton spoke in a very assuring voice, "You know that we should be more careful than we were this afternoon."

Ann Marie shyly replied, "If it happened, it will just have to happen. And, we'll elope and live happily ever after."

Barton grinned, "And we'll both go to school and live off my Dad's G.I. Bill plus what I can earn at some type of job or another, and the three of us will be a family."

Ann Marie smiled and asked, "Do we have to wait until I'm pregnant before we get married?"

Barton timidly replied, "No. We can declare ourselves as common law husband and wife like some folks do in the state of California and other places."

"Let's do it." Then she leaned over and said, "Let's wait about marriage, but let's do it."

Memories of his afternoon with her flashed across his mind and he wasted no time in nodding in the affirmative.

"The protection is in my car parked at your house." He then quickly added, "The drugstore is still open. We could walk over there."

Ann Marie laid a twenty dollar bill on the counter and asked the bartender to hold those sandwiches and that they would be back in about ten minutes.

The bartender smiled and waved his consent to them as they left the hotel, and walked the two blocks to Lanier's Drugstore.

Ann Marie waited in the shadows, out of sight of the Druggist she had known all her life. Barton went inside and requested one dozen Trojan condoms.

"That'll be three dollars." Then the Druggist inquisitively inquired, "Weren't you in here earlier this evening?"

Barton replied, "Yes sir."

He rejoined Ann Marie and told her about the Druggist questioning him.

"What did you tell him?" she asked as she gently slapped his shoulder.

"I told him that they were for a very dear, dear, lovable, loving, friend of mine."

They returned to the Inn Lounge where the bartender had their sandwiches ready. They ordered another beer each and two cold mugs and carried them upstairs to room 214.

At the door, he handed the sandwiches to Ann Marie, picked her up and carried her through the "threshold" and proudly stated, "In time I will do this officially. I love you Ann Marie Marbling."

CHAPTER 7

The Church

Barton had taken Ann Marie home at the suggested curfew of 10 o'clock and returned directly back to his room where he brushed his teeth, put on his pajamas and fell into the bed. He awoke at his usual 5:30, but remained in his bed thinking about the most lovable, most adorable girl that he had ever met. Not only was she a great lover, she was a great friend who seemed to know exactly how to make people feel very comfortable and at ease when in her presence. He loved Ann Marie Marbling.

He crawled out of bed and made his way to the bathroom and turned the water taps to fill the big tub. While the tub was filling, he brushed his teeth, shaved, then crawled into the warm water. He thought about the only girl with whom he had ever fallen in love. Most of his female contacts were usually in the presence of his parents, or Ebb, or Flossie who sometimes drove him and his dates to parties, but in almost every case, he was well chaperoned.

He had purchased the three pack of Trojans only because the boys in the fraternity thought it was a good idea to have them, just in case. But, he had never even used one before. Now, Ann Marie Marbling, the one girl who had made it easy for him, was also his first, and he knew that he was deeply in love with her. He grinned to himself and thought, "one of these days I am going to find out just how much loving that she can handle."

He got out of the tub and began drying himself as he looked into the mirror, with a pleasant expression, and said aloud, "She'd probably wear me down." Then added, "I am going to marry that young lady."

He glanced at his watch as he put it on his wrist, and noted, "I had best be going if I am to make the golf match with the Honorable Judge and his friends."

Dressed in his last clean pair of slacks, a white and blue slip over shirt, and penny loafers, he went down to the dining room to have breakfast.

Sylvester spotted him and motioned for him to join him for a second. He went over to Sylvester who was reaching into a closet. He brought forth a beautiful blue blazer which matched perfectly with Barton's khaki slacks. He held the blazer open so that Barton could put it on, and said, "Jackets are required in our dining room, so we keep a few around just in case a young man needs one so that he can enjoy a hearty breakfast."

He then winked at Barton and continued, "After your day yesterday, I expect you need some energy."

Barton hugged him and said, "Old friend. Wise friend. Good friend. You are so right."

He entered the dining room and spoke to almost everyone whom he passed, and he went to the table where Moses was already holding a chair. "Good morning, kind sir, and thank you," he said to the tall handsome black man dressed in his white shirt with silver vest, black trousers and shiny black shoes.

As he was about to be seated, he spotted Judge and Mrs. Marbling entering the dining room with Sylvester who was pointing toward Barton's table. Observing Sylvester's gestures in directing the Judge and Mrs. Marbling, Barton remained standing and waived to them to join him. The Judge came up and shook his hand, but, Mrs. Marbling hugged him, kissed him on the cheek, and remarked, "What a nice looking jacket."

Judge Marbling asked, "Have you ordered, yet?"

"No, Sir."

"Then let me order for you."

As the waiter was pouring coffee, the Judge spoke, "Sam, let's have three of the Salt Fish breakfasts." Sam nodded and continued pouring the coffee at the same time that Moses was placing orange juice on the table.

Mrs. Marbling looked motherly at Barton and said, "You look mighty spry and handsome this morning." She took a sip of coffee, looked over the rim of her cup and added, "I looked in on Ann Marie to see if she wanted to join us. She had a big smile and was certainly snoring, so I left her in bed." In the next breath, she again remarked, "That is a very pretty jacket."

Barton thanked her, took a sip of his orange juice, and asked, "May I tell you something in strictest confidence?"

They both smiled and simultaneously responded, "Why of course."

He squinted his eyes a little, then took a hesitating breath and said, "I'm in love with your daughter."

Judge Marbling raised his eyebrows and with somewhat of an approving smile, looked at his wife, then asked, "Does Ann Marie know?"

Relaxed, Barton responded, "I haven't told her yet." He continued, "There is an issue that I must clear with you, as I do not want to hurt Ann Marie in anyway."

The Judge looked concerned, gave a glancing askance gaze toward Mrs. Marbling and stated, "Pray tell us, young man, this issue which you want to clear with us."

Barton, with humble pride, stated, "I am a Catholic. I am a

devout Catholic, you are Baptist, and sometimes a difference in religious faith creates problems for some people where marriage is concerned."

The Judge asked, "What does Ann Marie say about this difference of religions?"

"We have not discussed it. I wanted to discuss it with you first because in most cases these problems occur with the parents." He spoke with a great deal of compassion.

He paused another moment and remarked, "Our children will be raised as Catholics, and if this presents a problem for you or for Ann Marie, then I will not ask her to marry me."

The Judge spoke in a somber, sympathetic tone, "That is a pretty hard fast rule. However, I know that it will not be a problem for me, and I don't think it will be for Mary Margaret." He put his arm on her shoulder and asked, "Will it?"

"Heavens no." Then she put her hand on Barton's shoulder and again gave him a motherly pat and said, "I am very much aware of some of the ridiculous superstitions that some people have about the Catholic religion." She paused, then continued, "To me religion is religion. Sometimes people confuse religion with a name."

She withdrew her hand from his shoulder and stated, "I have a dear friend who is a Catholic and she married a staunch Baptist. His mother showed her 'you-know-what,' and did indeed create problems for them until she learned that all the rest of his relatives had fallen in love with her and had accorded her the unofficial honor of being the prettiest girl in town."

Judge Marbling chimed, "True, true, indeed true. But the old girl really had a change of heart when she learned that her daughter-in-law was from a wealthy family." With a flirtatious smile for his wife, he said, "I was one of those who thought she was the second prettiest girl in town."

Mrs. Marbling smiled appreciatively at her husband and chimed, "That kind of remark will get you everywhere."

Barton smiled and thought "what a beautiful couple, no wonder Ann Marie is so gorgeous and lively." He then asked, "How did your friends handle the religious issue?"

"She and the children went to the Catholic church, and he continued to go to the Baptist." She continued, "And my young friend, the issue of religion will belong to you and Ann Marie, and not to me, nor her father, nor anyone else."

Sam was standing ready to serve the country breakfast and had heard Mrs. Marbling's thesis. He served the plates and when he got to Barton, he spoke, "And not even me, and you will be getting the second most beautiful girl in town, as I agree with the Judge on who is first."

Mrs. Marbling responded, "Why thank you, Sam."

Judge Marling smiled his approval of Sam's remarks and watched as Barton looked at his watch. It was almost eight o'clock. The Judge and Mrs. Marbling were having another cup of coffee, and Barton was drinking milk, when in walked DeNero, Maria, and Ann Marie.

Moses led them to the Judge's table and held the chairs for the ladies and pulled out a chair for DeNero.

The Judge and Barton were standing and had greeted them. They sat back down to finish their coffee and milk.

Ann Marie had not spoken a word. She kissed her mother on the forehead, then went around and kissed her father on the cheek. When she got to Barton, she reached down, picked up a small bite of biscuit with jam on it, and with defiant orchestration, stuck it into her mouth and began to chew in a manner whereby her jawls were puffed outward. She gave him a hearty bump with her arm, picked up his milk and guzzled it down.

Barton sat motionless with his eyes squinted and focused toward DeNero and Maria, and his lips slightly puckered as if to say, "This is my darling spoiled brat."

Ann Marie broke the silence and said, "Go on and play that silly game of golf. DeNero, Maria and I are going to Defuniak."

Barton stood. He moved his big brown eyes so close to hers that their noses were touching. She did not budge and inch. He pressed a little harder. She still did not budge. But when he said, "I love you," she melted and kissed his puckered lips. The whole crowd laughed in amusement at these two young lovers.

"I have time to sit with you while you have your breakfast."

She meekly replied, "I don't mean to make a fuss about you playing golf with dad and his group. I guess that I just don't want to share you."

He slipped off his gold ring with an amethyst stone flanked by diamonds on each side; took Ann Marie's left hand, and on her third finger, slid on the oversized ring and solemnly stated, "Another lady friend of mine gave this to me for my sixteenth birthday. The words of the birthday card were. 'Other than your father, you are the only living man that I will ever love.' It was post dated in Newfoundland. I never saw her again."

Tears were streaming down Ann Marie's cheeks, then she began to cry. He put her head on his shoulder and whispered into her ear, "Will you marry me?"

She began to bawl.

He took his handkerchief and began wiping her tears away and he knew that his love for her was genuine.

She took the handkerchief from his hand and started to wipe his tears away, but changed her mind and started kissing them away, and she knew that her love for him was genuine.

"You haven't answered my question," he prodded.

She recovered from her mournful thoughts about his parents, and in her natural and playful manner announced to all within normal hearing distance. "Yes, Barton Talmadge Sandeau, I will, this moment of this day, consent to be your wife."

Mrs. Marbling stood. The Judge stood. DeNero stood. Maria stood. And all at once the six of them were embraced.

The dining room was full of people, and when the word reached those who had not already heard the announcement, a round of applause broke out.

Ann Marie took her right hand and began to twirl the big oversize ring which Barton had put on her finger. She looked him in the eye, and with a mischievous smile, asked. "You will go to the wedding reception. Won't you?"

Apologetically, Barton replied, "I don't have a suit with me, and I have on my last clean pair of slacks. And, I have already scheduled the Stinson, and an instructor to give me a check ride so that I will be eligible to rent planes from Wards Aircraft."

Before Ann Marie could retort, the Judge remarked, "And you have your pilot's license?"

"Yes, sir." Then he spoke to Sam. "Please bring me the check and include these late sleepers."

Sam smiled at Barton and announced, "The Judge has already spoken and is now the proud holder of the check for the six of you." Everyone, in unison, thanked the Judge.

On the way out of the dining room, Ann Marie held her mother's elbow and quietly whispered, "Get Daddy to twist Barton's arm. I want to show up at the reception with him on my arm, and this big hunk of amethyst and diamonds on my finger."

Mrs. Marbling slightly scoffed, "My dear darling, my answer to that request is a big heartwarming no." Then she hugged her daughter and continued, "One: He does not have an invitation even though I am sure he would be welcomed; yet, he may feel as if he were imposing on your good friends."

Ann Marie hugged her mother again, "You are a big help." Then she winked at her and whispered, "I may just have a private reception for Mr. Sandeau, just as soon as he gets back from the airport."

Mrs. Marbling gave a not necessarily disapproving gasp as she joined the Judge. On their way out of the hotel, they spoke to Sylvester who had opened the door for them.

Seated in the car, the Judge inquired of his wife, "What was Ann Marie up to?"

Mrs. Marbling smiled seductively at her husband and quietly answered, "I think our daughter is about to know man."

The Judge looked at his wife and asked, "Are you in the mood to know man?"

Mrs. Marbling merely responded, "Lover, take me home."

At the table, in the dining room, Sam was serving the late sleepers. Barton excused himself and stated, "I'll go upstairs and finish getting ready. I'll be back shortly."

As he was leaving, he could hear Ann Marie mumbling, but could not make out what it was, so he continued out of the dining room and up the wide marble stairway to the second floor and to his room. When he returned to the dining room, the late sleepers had just about finished their breakfast. Barton sat beside Ann Marie and asked, "How do I get to the club?"

"I'll not tell." Then she laughed and told him. At one point in the directions she reminded him, "When you pass W.E. Shaw grocery, slow down because the right turn onto the club road is very close by and can hardly be seen if you are going fast. It is the first turn."

Chapter 8

The Golf

The directions to the club were easy to follow. A right turn on to Brundidge Street led him to a cybernetic intersection where a café sat in the southwest quadrant. He stopped a few seconds waiting for a traffic light to change, looked at Dorr's apartments on the northwest quadrant, thought that the architect on that building must have been in his tea when he designed it. It appeared to have a basic two-story rectangular building which had been added onto in every direction possible. It truly looked comfortable with its wide porch rambling into every nook wherever a door was found.

Diagonally across from Dorr's was a more orderly building, the Hilley Hotel, with its outbuildings of guests rooms.

The light changed to green. He put his car in gear and continued southward, also a segment of US Highway 231. The day before he had traveled this highway and had turned on to an Avenue that led him to the college.

He observed the many white dwellings, all which seemed to have been freshly painted, and all seemed to have well-manicured yards and neatly trimmed bushes, guarding porches, filled with high-back rocking chairs. At the end of this street, just before becoming the Elba Highway, was an impressive two-story, yellow brick house, with four large round columns extending from the ground level to the roof of the second floor.

"Wonder who lives there," he mused.

He came upon W.E.'s Grocery, slowed down, and began looking for the hidden turn that Ann Marie had told him about. He was glad that he had reduced his speed because the turn was upon him immediately. He stuck out his arm out of the window and gave a right-turn signal. About twenty yards onto this road, there was a group of young black boys. When they spotted his car, they came running.

He heard one cry out, "I'm the best caddy, choose me."

Just ahead, another car stopped and picked up a caddy, so he stopped. Most of the caddies rushed the car, but, standing apart from the yelling caddies, was a young man of about fourteen years of age. He was clean cut and looked like he would be a fine caddy. He motioned for the young lad to get in. He leaned over and opened the front door.

The lad looked a little puzzled at being invited to ride in the front seat. At first, he slumped as if he was hiding from someone.

"What is your name, young man?"

The young lad smiled and replied, "Arthur Bean, sir. What's yours?"

"Barton Sandeau."

"Mr. Sandeau, thanks for picking me today. I've never caddied before."

Barton smiled. "Don't worry. You'll do just fine. There will be three other caddies in our group. You observe them, or ask me. The main thing to remember is to be very quiet and still while the players are attempting their shots."

Arthur Bean straightened his posture, sat erect in the front seat, and said politely, "I'll be real quiet and still, and I'll learn to be a good caddy."

"I believe that you will."

Barton, with his brand new caddy sitting in the front seat — a tradition unknowingly being broken — drove through the gate, to the parking lot at the rear of the Deer Hill Country Club building, parked in an obscure place so not to interfere with parking spaces of the regular members. He opened the trunk, removed his clubs, shoes, and shag bag of balls.

"Arthur Bean, wait here with our equipment, I'll be back in a few minutes." He walked the short distance to the club house, inquired of a young man the whereabouts of the Pro Shop and was pertly told, "We ain't got one."

With this information, he proceeded through a rear door that opened into a narrow hallway about six feet long. The sign on the door on the right read: MEN'S LOCKER ROOM. The sign on the door on the left read: MEN'S REST ROOM. He entered to the right.

The locker room appeared to be about twelve feet square, jammed full of small metal lockers stacked on top of each other; small wooden benches lined the narrow space between the lockers. There was very little room to walk.

He spoke to several of the men, who were maneuvering in-between and over the benches. One was Mr. Paul Bydian who he met at the lodge the previous evening. "Mr. Bydian, have you seen Judge Marbling?"

Mr. Bydian, tying his shoelace, stopped and smiled, looking up at Barton, and said, "He's not here yet. He called me and told me that he had to take care of something at home, but would not be late for the match." He finished tying his shoes, stood up, offered his hand to Barton. "The Judge has already registered you; however, you do need to leave your dollar with Mr. Herring who is in the dining room."

He introduced Barton to the rest of the men in the crowded locker room. Barton waved to them as it was impossible to crawl over someone to shake hands.

Barton thanked Mr. Bydian, closed the door to the Men's Locker Room, continued down the short, narrow hallway, past THE BAR — a small nook which housed small open wooden cubicles that were full of various liquors. Each cubicle had a number on it. He thought, "Each person has his own private cubicle where he can leave his liquor." Two steps past THE BAR, he entered the dining room where he found Mr. Herring sitting at a table with a loose-leaf notebook in front of him, in which he was recording those registered for the day's play. Barton introduced himself, and placed a dollar on the table.

Mr. Herring took the dollar. "Good to meet you. You are in the foursome with Judge Marbling, Paul Bydian and Albert Rose and you will be teeing off last at the request of the Judge who claims he has something important to take care of at home." Then he laughed, "Welcome to Deer Hill."

"Thanks, Mr. Herring. Please tell me how much I should pay my caddy."

"Usually a dollar. And, if they do a good job, we normally give them an extra tip of fifty cents."

He thanked Mr. Herring, turned to the other men who were sitting about and introduced himself to each of them.

He left the club house, returned to Arthur Bean, who was cleaning the golf clubs. He had already wiped the shoes, and he had the shag bag out.

Barton smiled an approval of the efforts of his caddy, and told him to empty the shag bag and then move about a 100 yards down range and that they would warm up.

About every twenty steps, Arthur Bean would turn around, as

if to ask, "Is this one hundred yards?" And, each time, Barton would motion for him to get further down. Finally, Barton gave him the signal that he was at the desired spot.

Barton hit the first shag ball with his wedge.

Arthur Bean tried to catch it on the fly.

Barton laughed, motioned Arthur Bean to come forward to him. They met about half way. Barton explained the easy technique of shagging golf balls. Arthur Bean returned to the desired distance, and without any further help from Barton, instantly mastered the art of allowing the ball to hit the ground and then catching it on the first bounce and placing it into the shag bag.

He had hit about six or seven balls when a man came up and introduced himself as Albert Rose, and stated that he would be in the same foursome, and that he was looking forward to the match.

Barton shook his hand, asked if he would like to hit a few balls. Mr. Albert said, "Many thanks, but I've got to get ready." Then he added, "I'll see you at the first tee."

It was about 9:45 when Judge Marbling drove into the parking lot. He had a large lad sitting in the back seat. As his car stopped, the lad jumped out of the back door of the car and proceeded to open the front door of the car for the Judge. The large lad handed a pair of shoes to the Judge, took the clubs from the trunk, and appeared well acquainted with the Judge's routines.

The Judge spotted Barton and yelled, "Sorry, I'm late. Did you get squared away inside?"

Barton waved, motioned his head in the affirmative, and returned to hitting his shag balls. He hit a few more then motioned for Arthur to return. They put the shag balls into the trunk, and together walked to the putting green that was circular, and had a short walkway in each quadrant. Barton glanced at the sun and murmured, "One small walkway for each, North, South, East and West."

Mr. Albert, putting on the green, noticed Barton's attention to the short sidewalks and spoke, "This was once where the wind sock was located for a grass landing strip which ran down what is now number one fairway."

Barton laughed, shook his head in a friendly manner.

All twenty-four golfers gathered around the putting green. The order of play, called out by John Pierce, listed the Tillmans and the Castilles were first, since their schedule for the wedding required more time than the other foursomes who were not directly involved in the wedding. Finally, Mr. Pierce, jokingly, said, "Judge, your group is last. We did this just in case you needed more time at home this morning."

The Judge laughed, shook his head, turned to those gathered and spoke, "In case any of you have not met him, let me introduce Ann Marie's fiancé, Barton Sandeau."

Most all of the golfers waved a friendly hello to Barton, who was now standing beside Judge Marbling and the other members of his foursome.

When it came time for Judge Marbling's foursome to start play, Mr. Albert said, "Barton, since you're the guest, why don't you lead us."

Barton looked at the other members of his foursome as if to ask if his leading off met their approval. Each one gave him a hand motion to let her go. He stepped on to the tee, placed his ball a little on the right side, near the marker, took a waggle or two with his driver, addressed the ball, and stroked it about 240 down the fairway.

Judge Marbling smiled. Paul Bydian grinned his approval, as did Albert Rose. Then each one stepped to the tee and played his shot.

The foursome, with their caddies, began strolling down the fairway. The Judge told Barton, "We only have a nine-hole course. We hit from the white tees on the first round, then we hit from the blue tees on the second round."

The round was pleasurable for them. They carried on a little conversation in between shots, and the fact that each of them was stroking the ball with authority added a lot to the comradeship that was developing for Barton and his newfound friends. Their first round was six under par. Birdies on 1 (Mr. Bydian) Pars on 2 and 3. Birdie on 4 (Mr. Rose chipped in from about sixty feet). Barton contributed birdies on 5, 7, and 9. The second round team ball was five under par giving Judge Marbling's team a 61 for the day. The Judge was beaming. "That ought to get the cheese."

Barton grinned and explained to his playing partners that he did not have time to go into the clubhouse, that he had to be at the airport very soon.

The Judge responded, "You go ahead, I will collect your winnings for you."

Barton shook hands with Mr. Bydian and Mr. Rose and said, "I enjoyed the round." Then he shook the Judge's hand and said, "I'll see you later, sir." The three men watched Barton walk away, then they headed for the clubhouse and the small bar with the many cubicles.

At the car, Arthur Bean was sitting in the back seat. He had already cleaned the clubs as he had noticed the other caddies do. And, as Barton was taking off his golf shoes, Arthur Bean remarked, "Hand them back here to me and I'll clean them while we ride."

Barton handed him the golf shoes. "Where do you live?"

"Academy Street," announced the young lad proudly who had had a good day; he had learned to caddy.

Barton maneuvered the car out of the parking lot, drove to Academy Street, to the house designated by Arthur Bean, pulled to the curb, let him out, reached through the window, handed him two dollars, waved to his parents sitting on the porch and chirped, "You have a fine son."

CHAPTER 9

Check Ride

Barton left Academy Street and headed for the airport, arriving about twenty minutes before the appointed time.

He introduced himself to the lady behind the counter. She, in a very business-like tone, said, "I'm Mrs. Wards, the owner, and I understand from your phone call that you want to get checked out in the Stinson."

"Yes, ma'am. And the 182."

In a more casual tone, she said, "Our instructor phoned that he would be a few minutes late. The Stinson Station Wagon is on the ramp. You can preflight her if you want to go ahead." Without too much of a pause, she asked, "How do you want to pay for it?"

"Cash. Do I pay for it now?"

"No. We charge tack time hours, and that plane rents for $12 per hour." She hesitated, then added, "Wet."

He understood. That meant $12 which included the gas. So he remarked, "That's fine." He left the small office and its sole occupant, went to the ramp, walked to the Stinson Station Wagon, rubbed the leading edge of the canvas-covered elevator, and lingered a moment with his thoughts of flying with his mother in a similar airplane.

He checked the fuel, oil, and all moving parts visible from the outside, then he unbuckled the engine cowling and inspected the engine for any loose connections or any signs of oil leaks. There were none. The engine was very clean.

He was checking the propeller for any nicks when a man came up. "I'm Josh Cambers, your instructor."

Barton shook his hand, told him his name, handed him his log book, pilot's license, and current medical certificate, without being asked.

Mr. Cambers checked the pilots license, the medical certificate, and handed both back to Barton. He laid the log book in the pocket of the dash of the plane, backed out, asked, "Is she ready to go?"

"Yes, sir," he replied. He walked around to the pilot's side and crawled in.

Josh Cambers was already seated in the right side with his seat belt on.

Barton buckled his seat belt, closed the door, took out the check list, methodically proceeded to get the engines started, checked all gauges and controls, looked at Mr. Cambers and said, "We are ready to roll, Sir."

Mr. Cambers did not speak. Instead, he made a motion with his hand that was the signal to let her roll.

The check ride lasted almost an hour. Mr. Cambers was very thorough. When he was satisfied that Barton could handle the airplane, he told him to make the final landing an engine-out procedure.

Barton positioned the airplane for the final to Runway 32. Once in position, he cut the engine and let the plane glide toward mother earth. Enroute, he gently handled the trim tab to make the glide even smoother. The landing was almost perfect as the wheels touched the runway without any screech. The landing roll was about 200 feet, and just before she came to stop, he started the engine, gave her a slight right rudder, a little right aileron, and taxied her through the intersection back to the ramp.

Mr. Cambers took the log book from the pocket of the dash, opened it to the page of the next entry and wrote, "Check ride completed in a satisfactory manner."

The two pilots secured the Stinson on the ramp, walked into the office where Mr. Cambers gave Mrs. Wards the tachometer readings. She computed the time to be fifty minutes and quickly calculated the cost to be ten dollars.

Barton paid her the ten dollars and asked if he could reserve the Stinson for tomorrow for a trip to Tuscaloosa.

She looked at Mr. Cambers who smiled and reported, "He can handle it and he certainly knows his instruments."

"That settles it. She is yours for tomorrow."

Barton shook Mr. Camber's hand, asked about his fee, and paid him. "Thanks to both of you. I appreciate it," he said as he left.

He left the small office feeling pretty good at the events of this long day which still was not finished. He drove out of the parking lot, glanced at his watch, noted the time to be 5:45, and shrugged. "The wedding must be over."

He turned on to US 231 headed back to his hotel, had another thought, "I know a gorgeous young lady, perhaps a little spoiled young lady, who is still mad that I didn't go to the wedding with her, and who is going to be even madder when I tell her that I am going to fly to Tuscaloosa tomorrow, to see Aunt Alva."

CHAPTER 10

Ann Marie's Reception

Sylvester, with a big grin, met Barton as he entered the Inn door, shook his hand and handed to him a message which he had written.

"Call 1402," it said.

Barton read the message, looked at his friend and smiled. "Thanks."

He went to the counter with the two telephones, picked one up and asked the operator, "1402, please."

Ann Marie answered.

He asked in one of his rare, joking moods, "Is there one among you by the name of Ann Marie Marbling who jilted me in the third grade, and with whom I am still in love."

Before he could add anything else, Ann Marie started laughing and replied, "There is one among us who is going to pin your ears back if you don't get your dirty laundry and meet me in the lobby in about five minutes." She repeated, "I'll be there in five minutes."

Barton repeated, "In five minutes."

He put the receiver back into its cradle and stood the phone back on the counter, and hastily made his way upstairs to get his dirty laundry together.

Carrying the laundry bag over his shoulder, he descended the wide marble stairs into the lobby just as her Mercedes pulled to the curb and parked.

Already, Sylvester was at the curb, opening the door for Ann Marie.

Barton carried the laundry bag outside, threw it into the back seat, went around to Ann Marie, and kissed her on the cheek, as she stood in the street. A passing car tooted its horn. They both laughed.

He then spoke in his gentle tone, "Give me time to get a bath and dressed and I'll be over and we'll go to a movie, or do something."

Ann Marie winked and whispered, "I think I like the something better. Come to my house and and I will scrub your back . . . while you bathe."

Barton asked, "What about your parents?"

She winked again, "They decided to leave the reception and drive to the cottage at Grayton Beach." Then she very coyly added, "Mother had two glasses of champagne, and I thought that she was going to take my dad there in front of all those guests."

Barton laughed, "I don't believe that."

Ann Marie shyly stated, "I was teasing about her taking him there and then. But, I did hear her whisper to him that she felt the urge to get to the beach cottage."

Still standing in the street, Barton stroked her shoulder length hair, tickling her neck. "Let me get my shaving kit, and my car, and I will be on over."

She sighed. "If you don't mind, leave your car here. It will keep our nosey neighbors from wondering why your car was parked outside my house all night."

Barton looked pleased as he repeated, "All night?"

Ann Marie nodded. "All night and all day."

Without another word, Barton returned to his room, packed his shaving kit, started for the door, retreated to his dresser, picked up the remaining three packs of Trojans, put them in his pocket, hurriedly rejoined Ann Marie at her car and stated, "Let's go!"

"Hold up a second."

He walked to his car, checked to make certain that it was locked, then returned and crawled in beside Ann Marie. She said not another word as she drove to her house, parked in the garage, got out, closed the door, took the laundry bag from the back seat, proceeded to toss the washables into the washing machine at the rear of the garage, flipped the switch with a flare of "get going you little devil."

She went back to the car and gathered his dirty trousers and put them over her left arm, taking Barton's left hand leading him upstairs to the guest apartment.

Neither she, nor he, had said a word since leaving the curb at the Inn, and now, still no word as she placed his trousers on the table. Still nothing was said as she flipped her dress over her head and laid it on top of his trousers. With her back to him, she pointed to the snap of her bra.

Barton loved her foreplay games. He remained silent as he unsnapped her bra, kissed the small of her back, stepped out of his loafers, dropped his clothes to the floor and stood naked. He was ready.

Thirty minutes later with two Trojans spent, not a word was uttered. They lay on the thick bear rug in front of the sofa. She rolled over, kissed him, stood up, and without putting on any clothes, walked down the stairs to the laundry room.

Barton admired her every move as she descend the steps. He

thought to himself, "Her presence tends to remove all my loneliness. She is a pleasure to be with. I adore her."

He heard the dryer start up. He got out of bed and moved toward the stairs just as she arrived on the first landing.

She looked at him, maintained her fixed gaze, climbed the remaining steps, and walked right into his arms. Still in silence, she guided him to the rumpled bed.

The dryer stopped just as both had completely relaxed.

She whispered, "Lover, you now have clean clothes."

Barton kissed her nose. "Thanks, my adorable one."

He glanced at his watch, it was 7:15. He turned his eyes to look at Ann Marie, sat up in bed and shook his head, "What a gorgeous fiancée." He then politely stated, "Thank you for the clean clothes. Thank you for the something. And, now my chosen one, I am in need of a bath, and I am in need of some food."

She sat up in bed with her breast cupped under her folded arms, looked at Barton, sweetly chirped, "My dear husband-to-be. I love you. And I will now help you with your bath. After which, we will see about some food."

She jumped out of bed, slipped her dress over her head, noticing her panties which were still on the floor. She picked them up, stacking them with Barton's trousers. "You are not going over to the house naked, are you?" she chided.

He slipped on his pants, threw his shirt around his neck, stepped into his penny loafers, and sang, "Let's go." As they passed the laundry room Ann Marie fetched a pair of shorts, a T-shirt, and socks for Barton, moved through the side door of the garage apartment, walked the pathway to the house, entered through the screened portico and latched the door.

She took him directly to the bathroom of the master bedroom, opened the taps, let the warm water flow into the oversized tub, reached into the linen closet, brought forth a towel and wash cloth and handed them to Barton.

"I'll bathe across the hall."

Barton, soaking, enjoying the relaxation of his warm bath, observed the door gently open. In strode Ann Marie. "Actuallty, I think I'll bathe with you. The tub is big enough." She crawled in beside him.

The bath was refreshing. While drying each other with the large towels, Barton asked, "Where is a good place to eat?"

Without hesitating, Ann Marie blurted, "Smith's restaurant."

They left the bathroom, went into the bedroom and dressed. Ann Marie, in a loose fitting, organdy, low neckline dress, using very little makeup, no jewelry except the amethyst ring on her third finger, left hand, eyed her fiancé. "Am I overdressed?"

Barton, in his usual kahki pants, blue T-shirt, now clean, the ever-present blue blazer, brushed, and his shined penny loafers, replied, "Overdressed? No. You look great."

They entered Smith's Restaurant about eight o'clock

The Hostess, Mrs. Alice Smith, greeted them, "The only tables available are in the main dining room."

"That's fine, Mrs. Alice. I want you to meet my fiancé Mr. Barton Sandeau."

Mrs. Smith shook Barton's hand, said to Ann Marie, "I have already heard about Mr. Sandeau. And, I must admit that he is as handsome as your mother says."

Barton smiled and responded, "Thank you."

Mrs. Smith smiled, led them to a table in the center of the spacious dining room. As they passed the many patrons in the restaurant, Ann Marie acknowledged their silent greetings with a wave or a nod. She did not want to delay their dinner. They were hungry.

Before they were comfortably in their seats, a clerk, already at the table placing silver and glasses of water and fresh linen napkins along with two emblematic wine glasses, remarked, "Nice to have you with us, this evening."

Mrs. Smith motioned to Charles, a renowned waiter, making his way toward her with a carafe of Mr. J.D.'s private stock. A Vintage Chablis. He poured the wine and before he could open the menu, Ann Marie requested, "Two of the house special dinners, please."

Charles grinned and departed for the kitchen.

Barton nodded his approval, picked up the elegant, emblazoned wine glass, raised it to eye level, peered at Ann Marie and toasted, "To us. To our future. May it always be one of happiness and love."

Ann Marie gently touched her glass to his, spoke in one of her rare, sincere tones. "Growing up, I often dreamed about my knight in shining armor, and wondered what he would be like. When I spotted you at the Inn, and in the inebriated condition that I was, all of my dreams went up in smoke, and you were there. All my defense mechanisms went out the window. I wanted you then. I want you now." She slowly, without taking her eyes off of Barton, sipped her wine and added, "And, I want you forever."

A sparkle of light reflected in the amethyst stone on her finger. She squinted, raised the ring to her lips and caressed it.

Charles returned with dinners consisting of a small tossed salad, thinly sliced grilled fish, English peas, steamed carrots, corn muffin, and thinly sliced lemon cheese cake.

They ate very slowly, eyeing each other in between bites.

Occasionally, Ann Marie would twirl her ring.

Barton eased his hand onto hers and said, "I need to get you a ring that fits."

With a reflective tear in her eye, she said, "No other ring will ever mean as much to me as this one and the wonderful way in which you put it on my finger." She twirled the ring once more and asked, "Will you tell me about her?"

"She was beautiful. She didn't like to cook, no need. Flossie was always there. She loved flying. Her father taught her to fly, and she taught me to fly, it . . ."

He didn't get to finish. Many people, in the restaurant, preparing to leave, stopped by to speak to Ann Marie and to meet her fiancé. Barton found himself getting up and down as one after another would come by. He appeared pleased to be meeting so many people from Deer Hill, especially friends of Ann Marie's.

After several introductions, during a quiet time, he told Ann Marie about his planned trip to visit Aunt Alva, and he asked if she would like to fly to Tuscaloosa with him. She agreed even though she had never flown in a private airplane.

Charles brought the ticket which had been marked paid.

Barton gave him an inquiring look.

Charles pointed to one of the private dining rooms where Mr. Albert Rose and his party were dining.

After finishing their wine and dessert, the young couple got up and made their way to Mr. Albert's table in the private dining room, where they met the members of his party — most of whom they already knew, who were now congratulating Ann Marie on her engagement and giving Barton a pleasing scrutiny.

Barton thanked Mr. Albert for his generosity and again told him how much that he had enjoyed the golf match. Mr. Albert winked and remarked, "That golf match yielded enough for both our dinners."

Barton grinned, bid good evening to Mr. Albert and his party, then departed.

They left Smith's Restaurant and drove back to her house. He asked Ann Marie if he should put the car into the garage. She replied, "Yes. And, I want to go upstairs and make up that bed and pick up our clothes."

Barton drove the car into the garage and joined Ann Marie in the apartment. They changed the sheets on the bed and tidied the room, then went over to the main house.

They entered through the screened portico, and as Barton latched the door, he asked, "Where do I sleep?"

Ann Marie looked at him as if he had asked a foolish question, then replied, "With me, of course." She smiled and added, "And, as soon as mom and dad return, I'm going to see about making it official."

Arm in arm they ascended the steps to the bedroom of Ann Marie who pointed to the side of the bed next to the wall and said, "Your side."

It was almost eleven o'clock when both of them fell sound asleep; and, the next morning, Barton was still asleep when he felt Ann Marie crawl in next to him. Half awake, he put his arm around her.

He smelled fresh coffee.

He rolled over and made love to her without saying a word. They sat on the side of the bed looking at each other and sipping the lukewarm coffee.

It was well past his usual wake up time of 5:30. He glanced at his watch, broke the silence, and stated to Ann Marie, "Let's get dressed and get a jump on our trip to Tuscaloosa."

Ann Marie agreed and at the same time positioned herself for more loving.

Barton meekly stated, "I'm out of protection."

Ann Marie reached under her pillow and brought forth a Shiek and responded, "I noticed how many we had left so I borrowed one of dad's."

Barton shook his head slightly in an approving manner and allowed Ann Marie to sheath him with a Shiek.

CHAPTER II

Aunt Alva

Dressed and waiting for Ann Marie to complete her preparations, Barton walked down the drive to collect the papers which had somehow been overlooked. Returning with the papers, he waved to the lady on the porch of the house next door. He chirped a happy. "Good Morning."

The lady, dressed in morning cloak, hair curlers protruding about an untended face, a water pail in her hand, did not return his greeting. Instead, she gave him a very concerned look as if he had violated the pure and good conscience of her neighborhood.

She returned to her sprinkling of the many pots of ferns on her porch, then slowly, and slyly, eased her head back toward Barton to get another look

Barton ignored her and continued back to the house with the papers.

He met Ann Marie coming out of the door, looking refreshed in her denim skirt, red-and-white striped shirt, blue ribbon holding her hair back, exposing her beautiful face with moderate makeup, and open toe sandals with no socks.

Barton gave her an adoring look, suggested that she change her footwear to socks and tennis shoes, as the temperature would be a little cooler once they were high in the air.

Ann Marie, being observed by the lady in the curlers, waved

to her. "Good Morning, Mrs. Langur." Still no response.

Ann Marie went back into the house, hurriedly changed her footwear, returned to the porch, grabbed Barton's arm, and rushed him to the car, as she handed him the keys.

He backed the car out, turned it around, headed down the drive to the street. All under the watchful eye of Mrs.Langur, still in her morning cloak and curlers, and still trying to figure out the situation.

Ann Marie, again, waved.

Mrs. Langur, flurried hurriedly back into her house without returning the wave.

"Who in the world is that beauty?" Barton asked.

Ann Marie laughed, "You don't want to know." And, in her joking pantomime, told him that the lady in the morning cloak, the lady in her curlers, the lady with the barren face, the lady who was a nosey rosy, the lady who was a vigilant, observing neighbor, was reputed to have seduced an elderly bachelor doctor; and, the story continues that the doctor, in his seventies, did in fact die of a heart attack while they were making love.

Barton joked, "Maybe he went happy." He quickly added, "Erase that. That remark was in bad taste."

Grinning her understanding, Ann Marie suggested that they get a bite of breakfast.

Nothing else was spoken. He drove toward the Motor Court and Café. After parking the car, he sat for a moment admiring Ann Marie, marveling at the way she had filled a deep void in his life, since his parents expired. "Let's get that breakfast," he said, opening the door.

They entered the café. At the very first table, sat Mr. Albert Rose, Mr. Paul Bydian, his brother, Jarvis, and Mr. John Pierce.

Mr. Albert said, "Good morning, what are you two up to this

beautiful day?"

Ann Marie proudly announced, "We're going to fly by private plane to Tuscaloosa to visit Barton's Aunt Alva."

Jarvis Bydian dropped his fork and began to choke.

Paul Bydian, slapped him on the back, gave him a very discerning look, and waggled his head.

John Pierce shook his head and gave Jarvis a smirked look.

Barton sensed some peculiarity, but asked Mr. Albert, "You playing golf today?"

"Right. We're getting an early start so that we can go to the baseball game this afternoon. A young rookie, called 'Fireball' is pitching for the Andalusia team in our Class D League."

Barton gave a slight motion with his hand, bid them to have a good round of golf, moved with Ann Marie to the table where the clerk was waiting with a tray of coffee cups, pot of coffee, silverware, and two glasses of water.

As Barton was assisting Ann Marie with her chair,the clerk inquired, "Coffee?"

Both replied, "Yes, ma'am."

To the open menu on the table, Barton pointed, then asked Ann Marie, "Want the breakfast special?"

"Suits Me."

The clerk merely called, "Two specials."

Ann Marie sipped her coffee, smiled, looked past Barton to the table where Jarvis Bydian had almost choked when she told them that they were flying to Tuscaloosa to visit Barton's Aunt Alva.

She was in curious thoughts. First, old lady Bydian fainting at the lodge when she first saw Barton, and now her bedeviled son almost choking when Aunt Alva was mentioned. And, she thought about Sara Lou Bydian's comment.

"Grandmother has this fixation of guilt about not letting Jarvis marry the girl who was pregnant with his baby."

Ann Marie's clever mind was working hard when Barton asked, "Penny for your thoughts."

Before she realized, she spoke aloud, "Could there possibly be a connection?"

"What are you talking about? What connection?"

She did not answer.

The clerk placed on their table, two glasses of orange juice, and two plates with bacon, eggs, grits, and hot biscuits.

They ate in silence for a few minutes, then Barton asked again, "What connections were you thinking about?"

In her well-executed evasive manner of pointing in one direction, then to another, she merely replied, "Just some private thoughts of mine."

Barton laughed. "Well, gather your little private thoughts and let's get on our way."

He held her chair for her to get up, gave her a stern but lovable look and said, "Don't play games with me, young lady."

On their way out, they passed the table where Mr. Albert, the Bydians, and Mr. Pierce had been sitting. Ann Marie noticed a crumpled napkin.

On the crumpled napkin was scribbled one word: Alva.

She picked it up.

She put her arm in Barton's as they walked out the door. As they drove toward the airport, they listened to a radio broadcast announcing that an inquest of Clarabelle Bradleton's death would be held on Monday at 10 A.M.

Funeral plans had been duly postponed pending an autopsy requested by her sister, Mrs. Maudie Jefferson, who believed that there was foul play involved in her sister's death.

Barton pulled into the parking lot of the airport, cut off the radio, engine, got out, went around, opened the door for Ann Marie, and helped her out.

They walked into the small office, greeted Mrs. Wards, who congratulated Ann Marie on her forthcoming marriage; at the same time, she pushed a form toward Barton, and proceeded to tell Ann Marie, "Mr. Cambers says that your fiancé is a good pilot, so you should enjoy your flight, today."

Ann Marie thanked Mrs. Wards, exited the small office, followed Barton to the tarmac, to the ramp where the Stinson was tied down. It had been washed and looked almost new.

Barton looked admiringly at his fiancée. "Come on. This is your first lesson about flying."

He clearly pointed to each item in the check list, and, very slowly, explained its function. When the outside preflight was finished, he opened the door on the right side, helped her to get seated, showed her how to buckle the seat belt in the proper position.

He closed the door and latched it, leaving the window open so the cockpit would be reasonably cool, while he walked around the airplane once more to double check the aileron and elevator connections.

Satisfied that all the hinges would stay put, he climbed into the cockpit, picked up the checklist, handed it to Ann Marie, saying "Start with number one, read it aloud. Watch me perform that particular function, then go to number two, and so on."

Going over the check list so slowly took a little longer than usual, but Ann Marie's interest was so keen that Barton carefully explained each function and how it related to the total performance of the airplane.

Once ready, Barton announced over the unicom, "Deer Hill

traffic, Stinson Four Eight Three Alpha George taxing to runway 25 for IFR departure Tuscaloosa."

He told Ann Marie to put her feet on the rudder peddles and just let them ride there and that she would get the feel of what he was doing with them.

He taxied the short distance to the run-up apron, stopped the plane, pulled on the brakes, leaned across Ann Marie, closed and latched the window. As he started back, he kissed her on the nose, winked, and said, "We'll be off shortly."

He eased the throttle inward until the gauge read 1700 rpm, twice checked the magnetos, continued with all the other pre-takeoff procedures, which he explained. He picked up the mike and announced, "Deer Hill traffic, Stinson Four Eight Three Alpha George departing runway 25 , IFR, Tuscaloosa." He then did his clearing turns and taxied on to runway 25.

With the nose aligned with the runway center line, he notched ten degrees of flaps, increased the power slightly, peered across the panel to check that all gauges were reporting normal, pushed the throttle to full power, and began rolling. About midfield, the Stinson rotated off the runway and into the beautiful clear blue sky.

He maintained the runway heading of 25, climbed to 800 feet, made a 90 degree climbing turn to the south, reached 1200 feet, made a 45 degree climbing turn to the west, put the plane into a smooth climb, standard rate turn northward to intercept his on course heading to the Montgomery VOR. Reaching 2000 feet altitude, he switched radio frequency to Montgomery, called, "Montgomery Radio, Stinson Four Eight Three Alpha George, out of 2000 for 4000 inbound on 160 radial."

Ann Marie listened carefully as a voice came over the speaker, "Good Morning Stinson Four Eight Three Alpha George report reaching 4000. We have your clearance when ready."

Barton took his pencil and prepared to copy his clearance. When finished he read it back. The Montgomery Controller responded, "Read back correct. Report over Montgomery at 4000."

Ann Marie was interested in everything that took place on her maiden flight in a private airplane, and she had no problem remaining silent. She listened carefully to every word that came over the radio.

Barton had flown the airplane to the assigned altitude of 4000 feet, began to explain the effects of the trim tab, when the needle of the VOR began to fluctuate. He explained that this indicates that the airplane is positioned near the Montgomery station. He picked up the mike, reported, "Stinson, Four Eight Three Alpha George, over Montgomery, 4000, Fourteen Zero Six Zulu."

"Roger, Alpha George, Montgomery Altimeter 30.02"

"Thirty point zero two. Alpha George," repeated Barton, then turned to radial 328 outbound. "The Controller resolves all conflicts," he explained, "of airspace and we are committed to maintaining our assigned heading and altitude."

After a while, she spoke. "Tell me about Aunt Alva."

Barton made a little abrupt course correction that brought Ann Marie's eyes upon him. "You have a right to know. Aunt Alva, my daddy's sister, went through a very traumatic venture which caused her to go insane." He paused and methodically pointed to each of the gauges and proclaimed, "All systems okay." Then solemnly continued, "The story that I was told is that she was in love with this boy who was a frequent visitor to her school, Orion Female Institute, and that he purportedly wanted to marry her. Anyway, she got pregnant. The boys mother wouldn't permit him to marry her, and did indeed, fabricate a story that he had run away, joined the Army, or was it the Foreign Legion.

"She told Aunt Alva's family that she did not know how to get in touch with him; when, in fact he had actually been sent to Florida to live with relatives until this affair blew over. Her parents, my grandparents, were so upset, and embarrassed, that they sold their farm, moved with Aunt Alva to Jefferson County where she gave birth to a baby boy."

He paused again to make a slight course correction and to do a routine panel check, frowned, became solemn, and stated, "At the birth of her baby, she went into a trance and has not been out of it since. My mother and father, as far back as I can remember, would take me every third Saturday to Tuscaloosa, to Brice's Hospital, to visit with her. She never says one word to us. When we walk in, she smiles, and begins singing verses of the song ' The Spanish Cavalier.' After a few verses, she returns to her glazed stare, grabs the arms of her rocker, stiffens her entire body until it becomes very rigid. The staff at the hospital says that the only time that she smiles or utters any words is whenever we visit."

Their conversation about Aunt Alva was interrupted by the Controller at Montgomery, who handed them off to Birmingham, who acknowledged contact, and gave them the altimeter reading.

When it was all done, Ann Marie asked, "Where is her baby?"

Barton shook his head and answered, "He died at an early age. I don't remember him. Mother always told me that we were born so close together that we were almost like twins."

A voice came over the speaker, "Stinson Four Eight Three Alpha George, report Tuscaloosa Airport, in sight."

Barton acknowledged the transmission about the time that

Ann Marie spotted the buildings of the University of Alabama. Off the right wing, they could see Denny Stadium, and on the nose, the Black Warrior River; and a little beyond, to the west, was the Airport.

Barton keyed the mike, reported, "Birmingham Radio, Stinson Four Eight Three Alpha George, we have a visual, Tuscaloosa Airport, please close our IFR."

"Roger, Stinson Four Eight Three Alpha George altimeter 30.05. Good Day."

Barton acknowledged the altimeter reading, switched frequency to Tuscaloosa Unicom, gave them a call, and proceeded to land runway 22, as advised.

With Ann Marie's feet again on the rudder pedals, Barton taxied to Bama Air where they were met by a young attendant who guided them into a tie down space, then came up and asked what services that they would be needing.

"Top her off with 80 octane, oil to six quarts, and if time permits, hit my windshield a lick." They deplaned. As they passed the lady in the office, he asked her if she would be kind enough to call him a cab—he wanted to go to Brice's Hospital.

They boarded the cab in front of the Van de Graff building, advised the driver of their destination, then slumped back into the seat.

The cab driver was inquisitive, asking too many questions about flying, about who was at Brice's, and about Alabama football. In all cases, Barton politely responded with very little information.

The cab entered the drive of the hospital and stopped at the gate. Barton handed his pass to the security guard who gave it a brief inspection, and signaled the cab into the fenced compound. The driver stopped in front of the designated building, got out, opened the door for Ann Marie. Barton paid the fare plus tip and asked, "We will only be a few minutes. Can you wait?"

The driver stated that he could wait fifteen minutes without any further charge.

"Appreciate it," echoed Barton. He put his arm around Ann Marie to reassure that everything would be okay with the visit with Aunt Alva. They entered the front door, into a hall, where the duty nurse, recognizing Barton, said, "Same room."

He logged his and Ann Marie's name in the register and took her by the arm, and went straight to room 128. At the door, he hugged her around the shoulder, quietly opening the door to Aunt Alva's room. They remained standing as they went inside. Aunt Alva glanced over her shoulder, smiled, and began singing:

> A Spanish Cavalier stood in his retreat,
> and on his guitar played a tune, dear.
> The music so sweet, he would oft time
> repeat to his country, and to you my dear.

She sang two more verses, returned to her stolid expression, grabbed the handles of her rocker, and stretched her body until it became rigid.

The entire episode took all of three minutes.

Barton, still holding Ann Marie's hand, led her out of the room without saying anything at all to his Aunt. They moved back down the hall, logged out, went outside, motioned the cab driver, turned for another look at the building of Aunt Alva. "Back to the Airport, please," he said, mildly as he he got into the cab.

The cab driver, sensing that his conversation would not be

needed, went about his business of maneuvering through the traffic and to the airport.

Barton and Ann Marie held hands for the entire trip. The only words spoken were Ann Marie's query. "Why does she have a smile only for you?"

Before he could muster an answer, the cab stopped in front of the Van de Graff building at the airport. They got out and paid the fare plus a tip for waiting at the hospital and bid the cab driver goodbye.

They stood facing each other in the bright sunshine. He answered her query. "The story that I was told is that she believes that she killed her baby. When I show up, she does a reversal, and believes that I am the baby who was supposed to have been killed. So, she smiles and sings her song."

Ann Marie kissed him on the cheek.

He smiled, took her hand, and led her into the office, paying the gas bill of $3.40. He asked her quietly, "Do you need to go to the rest room?"

He was almost finished with the pre-flight of the plane when Ann Marie joined him. "I feel better," she said.

The return enroute flight was pretty much routine, and the conversation was mainly about their hopes and dreams. They were over the Alabama River, heading home.

Barton ask the name of the jewelry store where Mr. Claude worked.

"Dorrough's Fine Jewelry," she said.

Montgomery Radio requested, "Stinson Four Eight Three Alpha George. Say your position." Barton responded, "Over Montgomery VOR, 3000. turning outbound 140 radial in-bound Deer Hill."

His next words over the radio advised Montgomery that he

had Deer Hill Airport in sight, and requested that they cancel his IFR flight plan, which they did with a parting, "Good Day." He contacted Deer Hill unicom. Mrs. Wards advised, "Runway 25 is the active. We have other traffic, shooting touch and goes."

He positioned his plane for the approach, advised Deer Hill traffic that he was entering a right base for 25. Someone else, unannounced, at a lower altitude, was also turning on a base leg for 25.

Barton keyed his mike, "Cessna 150, turning base for 25, please state your intentions."

An instructor came on. "Sorry about that. We'll go around."

Barton reduced his power, pulled 10 degrees of flap, made his procedure turn to final, further reduced power, added another 10 degrees of flap and let 483AG glide smoothly to mother earth.

A small group near the hangar observed the landing. It was almost perfect. It crossed the thresh hold at fifty-four miles per hour with an altitude of fifty feet, then eased onto the runway, stopped at the first intersection and taxied to the fuel pumps.

He did his post-flight cockpit check. Satisfied that all systems were off, he recorded the tachometer time, and got out of the plane. Ann Marie had already gotten out and headed for the rest room.

Barton started for the small office, but was hailed by Mr. Cambers, his checkride instructor, who came over. "Sorry about that Barton. Our mike was acting up."

"No problem." He went inside and paid Mrs. Wards the $32.60 rental fee. He thanked her and met Ann Marie coming out of the restroom.

"Be with you. In a minute."

"I'll go get the car and wait for you."

It was exactly 12 o'clock when she drove the Mercedes on to

US 231, headed toward town. In a very short distance, she and
Barton came upon a big eighteen wheeler. She followed it, as
there was no place to go around. Patiently, she remained behind
the truck until it turned into the parking lot of the Motor Court
and Café.

Barton suggested, "Follow that truck, we'll eat the vegetables
at the café."

She quickly wheeled the Mercedes into the parking lot, and
remarked, "Yep. Let's get the vegetables." She parked the car,
reached over and put her hand on Barton's thigh. As serious as
she could possibly be, added, "Let's spend the afternoon loving
and talking about our marriage."

"A darn good idea. But let's eat first."

The clerk who had served them breakfast, motioned for them
to sit at the counter where there were a few vacant stools.

They either spoke or waved to almost everyone in the building even though Barton did not know many of them; however,
they knew who he was. He was Ann Marie's fiancé.

They finished lunch, paid the fare, and went to the Mercedes,
whereupon he opened the driver's side door for Ann Marie.
"Let's get to the jewelry store."

In her playful, amorous, anticipatory mood, she saluted,
"Aye, aye, sir."

She drove to the square and found a parking space near the
Court house located in the center, guarded by a statute of a
Confederate Soldier facing North.

She noticed Barton's attention to the statute. "He did a good
job. Not one Yankee soldier ever set foot on Deer Hill soil."

He laughed, put his arm around her shoulder and headed
across Elm Street to the jewelry store.

Inside they found Mr. Claude as Barton had hoped. He had

met him at the golf course when he played with the Judge.

He shook Mr. Claude's hand and told him that he wanted to buy a ring for Ann Marie. Mr. Claude unlocked the heavy glass cage and reached in, bringing forth a tray of diamond rings.

Barton looked soberly at Ann Marie. "Which one do you like?"

She kissed him on the cheek. "Kind sir, that is your choice to make. So make it while I look around."

Barton selected the ring, handed it to Mr. Claude who took his binocular, inspecting it for any flaw. He then summoned Ann Marie. "Come here, lucky one, and get fitted for this piece of ice."

Ann Marie rushed to the counter and stuck out her hand.

Mr. Claude motioned for her to remove the amethyst and hand it to him and he would clean it. "Nice ring," he stated.

He handed the selected diamond to Barton and mootly gestured, "Put it on her."

He took the previously ringed third finger, left hand, and slipped the Diamond on.

It fit perfectly.

Ann Marie started to remove the diamond, assuming that Mr. Claude would keep it until his check cleared. But Mr. Claude stopped her and remarked to Barton, "Write your check. No way that you are going to run out on this beautiful, spoiled daughter of the Judge."

She was admiring her diamond when Mr. Claude handed her the amethyst which his aide had cleaned. She put the amethyst on the third finger, right hand, held both hands up and looked Mr. Claude in the eye. "Will you marry this spoiled brat to that spoiled brat?"

Mr. Claude grinned, took Barton's check without even

looking at it, and remarked, "I expect that we best find someone who can do it legal; and, I expect that we best wait for the Judge and Mrs. Marbling."

CHAPTER 12

The Club

They left the jewelry store, practically skipped back to the parked Mercedes, and waved to a few friends on the street, all under the watchful eye of the Confederate Soldier.

Ann Marie stumbled slightly a couple of times admiring her ring instead of watching her step. Barton slowed down and took her right arm, freeing her left hand to be admired as she walked. "I want to go home, right now," she said.

Giving her an eager expression, he asked, "Take me to my car. I need to get something."

She crawled into the driver's seat, started the engine, propped both hands on the steering wheel, admired her glistening rings, flexed her fingers, looked at Barton and cranked the engine.

Finally she drove out of the parking lot, giving the Confederate Soldier a left handed salute. "Take care old friend."

Barton said not another word until she pulled in beside the 1933 Plymouth, parked at the Deer Hill Inn. He jumped out. "I'll only be a second."

He unlocked the passenger side door, reached into the camel hair-covered pocket, brought out the dozen Trojans he had purchased earlier and stuck them into his pocket.

He whispered to Ann Marie, "Now, we can go to your house."

"Want it be nice when we can say 'our house.' And, want it be nice when we don't have to be concerned about Trojans."

Barton only gazed at her, in admiration of her beauty, and her brains. In three days, he had met a person perfect for him. She joked a lot. She clowned a lot. She had very few, if any, hang-ups. She was an adorable doll. He loved this beautiful creature.

She gave the turn signal, drove on to College Street, puckered her lips, looked at Barton, leaving no doubt that she loved him.

He smiled, pretending that he did not understand. He followed Ann Marie upstairs to the apartment, as they got out of the car.

She wasted very little time getting her beloved fiancé into the double bed. In an hour they were sound asleep and snoring.

Aroused by a familiar shuffle down stairs, Ann Marie yelled, "I'll be down in a minute, Roxy."

She slipped on her house cloak and went down the stairs of the garage apartment. At the landing, halfway down, she met Roxy coming up with an armload of Barton's trousers that she had cleaned and pressed. Roxy rolled her big eyes, twitched her lips, looked straight at Ann Marie, "Honey child, I know that you're grown, but in the middle of the day!"

Ann Marie scoffed, flashed her diamond, then the amethyst, hugged Miss Roxy. "I'm in love."

Roxy put her heavy arm around Ann Marie. "That makes a difference. Just make sure he's not just fooling you."

Ann Marie looked Roxy in the eye, flashing her diamond. "At the price he paid for this piece of ice, and if he is just fooling around with me, he has made me the highest priced . . ."

Before she could finish, Roxy said, "Hush child." Then she walked down the stairs and out of the garage apartment.

Ann Marie climbed the stairs with Barton's trousers hanging

over her arm, putting them in the closet. She turned to Barton
and flirtatiously chimed, "I might as well start moving you in,
shirt by shirt, because we'll be living here just as soon as I can get
with mom and dad."

They had been asleep about three hours before Roxy awakened them. Barton looked at his watch. It was 6:30. He looked
admiringly at something else, his fiancée. She dropped her house
cloak to the floor, picked up a towel and strolled naked into the
small bathroom.

He could hear the water running into the small tub. He could
hear Ann Marie humming the tune "A Spanish Cavalier" over
the rushing water.

He folded his hands under his head, thought about the many
things that he needed to get done before his wedding.

He needed to open a bank account in Deer Hill. He needed
to lease his house or sell it. "Ebb and Flossie would be put out,
though" he thought, "so I better just lease it." He needed to
check with the Veteran's Officer at the college and get transferred the G.I. benefits that he had inherited from his father. He
needed to get back home, get his belongings. His thoughts went
on and on until he was interrupted by a gorgeous female leaning
over him. She kissed him on the nose. "Will you take me to the
club for dinner, tonight? Most of the members, and their virgin
daughters, will be there. I want to show off my pretty diamond
ring. And, I want them all to see the pretty stud that I am to
marry."

Barton crawled out of bed and strode naked into the bathroom. He took only ten minutes to brush his teeth, shave, and
bathe. He returned to the bedroom, where Ann Marie was
dressed and brushing her lovely black hair.

"Wow!" Barton whistled. "I need to take you home and show

you off to my buddies. But, I'm afraid that they will take you away from me."

Ann Marie, with the look and walk of a belly dancer, moved toward him. "No one will take me away from you."

He kissed her on the neck, and continued with his tie.

They drove leisurely to the club. As they were getting out, Mr. Albert Rose parked alongside. He waved to Barton to hold up a minute. He opened the door for his guest.

Ann Marie called Miss Annie, Mr. Albert's guest, over to her, showed her the diamond on her left hand, then hugged her.

Mr. Albert and Barton were observing Ann Marie's and Miss Annie's little embrace when Ann Marie turned and said, "And I want you to meet my main man."

Miss Annie laughed, "Well, don't I get a hug from your main man."

Barton hugged Miss Annie. "It is truly my pleasure to meet you and I hope that we get to see more of you."

"How was your flight, today?" Mr. Albert asked.

"Wonderful. That's the way to travel." Then she asked, "Are you two, alone? If so, we would love to have you as our guests for dinner."

Mr. Albert replied, "We are alone. And, we will happily join you for dinner. And, I'll pay the tab. And, Barton, I hope, will agree to fly me in that airplane to Greenville, Mississippi, sometime."

Barton laughed. "I certainly will take you to Greenville. But there is no need for you to treat us again. And, we certainly appreciate your treat at Smith's."

Mr. Albert responded, "I'm a bachelor who gets a great deal of pleasure entertaining my friends, so that's the end of that."

"So be it," remarked Ann Marie. She took Miss Annie's arm,

and the four of them walked arm in arm through the parking lot, into the entrance foyer of the club where they were met by James, the maitre' d.

"The dining room is buzzing, and I think you and Miss Ann Marie would like to have dinner in the bar area," he whispered to Mr. Albert.

Miss Annie inquired, "James, what's all the buzzing about?"

James glanced, noticed that Ann Marie and Barton were out of hearing range. "Oh! Miss Annie. Ole Miss Bydian was in one of her ornery moods, seemed to get quite irritated with Mr. Jarvis. Finally, Mr. Paul got her to leave. She was besides herself. She's got this notion that Miss Ann Marie's fiancé is the illegitimate son of Mr. Jarvis. She wants to find out for sure, regardless of who it hurts. That's what all the buzzing is about."

Ann Marie, with Barton at her side, had not heard James's reason for the buzzing. She was very much enjoying introducing her fiancé to the many people coming and going.

And, no one missed the diamond on her third finger, left hand; nor, the oversized amethyst on her third finger, right hand.

Sara Lou Bydian, whose grandmother was always shoving her into social events of the young and wealthy, never letting her be herself, certainly did not miss seeing the rings. She was holding Ann Marie's left hand, wooing about it. Then as if she had been struck by something, she squealed in her haughty little voice, "Oh! Ann Marie, if what my grandmother says is true, your fiancé and I may be cousins." Then she smirked as though her grandmother was prompting her. "Illegitimate of course."

Ann Marie, in a perfectly calm manner, responded, "Which of you is illegitimate?"

Miss Annie put a napkin to her mouth to control her laugh.

Mr. Albert gave an approving "Huh! Huh!"

Sara Lou Bydian tucked her tail and fled.

Miss Annie spoke, "Barton, I want to apologize to you for the whole damn town."

"Miss Annie, there is no need for an apology. I have no idea what possesses Ole Miss Bydian, and I have certainly met a thousand Sara Lou Bydians in my day. So, if it meets with everyone's approval, let's enjoy our evening."

James brought a bottle of Cabernet, proceeded to pour without anyone doing the sampling honors. Miss Annie said, "James knows that we enjoy that wine, so we don't bother with the sampling.

The four were having fun toasting when Mr. Paul Bydian came into the room, with Sara Lou holding on to his arm.

He said in a very quiet voice, "Albert, ladies and gentlemen, Sara Lou has something that she would like to say, if it is all right."

"Certainly, Sara Lou, what news do you bring?" Albert asked as he stood.

Barton, already standing as Mr. Bydian was speaking offered Sara Lou his chair.

She politely refused and began, "To all of you, I want to apologize for my behavior earlier."

Barton stopped her, put his arm around her shoulder, spoke, "Sara Lou, I would be honored to have you for a cousin regardless of my situation; however, my parents lived together for a long time, not to be married."

Ann Marie, sensing Sara Lou's embarrassment, got up, moved next to her, put her arms around her, whispered, "Let's forget. And remain friends."

Mr. Bydian spoke, "Thank all of you. We're sorry that we interrupted your toast." He was about to say something else, when James appeared with two wine glasses, handed one to Mr. Bydian, the other to Sara Lou.

Sara Lou looked quizzical toward her father as if to ask his permission to have a glass of wine, then spoke, "What will grandmother say about this?"

Mr. Paul took her glass and handed it to James and said, "Please, Mr. James, pour."

James poured, returned the partially filled glass to Mr. Paul, who handed it to Sara Lou, and remarked, "My darling daughter, you are nineteen, and I think that it is time that you stop allowing my mother, your grandmother, to keep you from having some fun. So, I offer a toast to Mr. Sandeau and his lovely fiancée, and to Mr. Albert and Miss Annie, and to my only child, Sara Lou, who is about to have her first encounter with the grapes."

Mr. Paul Bydian held Sara Lou's hand steady for her to hold the wine glass, then bowed. He then added, "Miss Sara Lou, I think you are grown enough to partake of the grapes, and what better occasion than to toast the engagement of Ann Marie and Mr. Sandeau."

The crowd in the bar area, who had heard Mr. Paul Bydian's approval speech, began a slight applause.

Still standing, Albert held his wine glass about eye level and said, "A toast to two young lovers, Barton and Ann Marie."

James was standing nearby with a trey holding the four dinners of lobster and filet. He yelled, "Hear! Hear! Now let's eat."

Someone had summoned the musical ensemble from the dining room and they were situated in a corner playing the tune, "What a Wonderful World."

Albert, Barton, Miss Annie, and Ann Marie stood, saluted the three-piece musical group. James returned with another bottle of Cabernet, compliments of Sara Lou Bydian.

Miss Annie leaned toward Ann Marie, whispered, "It is amazing, the pleasant effect that a few smashed grapes can bring about."

Ann Marie, sipping her wine, whispered in Miss Annie's ear, "Especially when the haut monde becomes hauteur and not haute nor naught te."

Miss Annie almost dropped her glass.

The four friends ate slowly while they wrestled expertly with the lobster, and filet, consumed the third bottle of Cabernet, and for all intent and purpose, shook the hands of everyone in the building.

Mr. Albert signed the tab for the dinner, leaving a cash gratuity for the staff, and began leaving the bar. He introduced Barton to several people as they waited for Miss Annie and Ann Marie, who had stopped at a table or two on their way out.

Near the door, Miss Annie asked Ann Marie, "Where did you learn to handle the booze?

Ann Marie hugged her and replied, "Booze 101, Randolph."

Miss Annie hollered, slapped Ann Marie on the back, remarked, "At least you learned something."

They went to the parking lot, graciously thanked once more Mr. Albert for a very fine dinner, said good night to Miss Annie, got into their car and drove home.

CHAPTER 13

The Mass

The sun, brightly shining through the upstair window of the garage apartment, beamed in Barton's eyes. He squinted one eye, looked at his watch and saw that it was 5:30. Ann Marie's head was resting on his chest; she was "sawing logs." It was the same type snore that he had heard, in his room, at the Deer Hill Inn, the day he first met her.

He rolled over, kissed her on the forehead and softly whispered, "If you're going to Mass with me, you'd better wake up."

She opened one of her big blue eyes. "Why do they have Mass during the night?"

Barton laughed, "It is at 7 A.M." He jumped out of bed and headed for the bathroom.

At 6:30, both were dressed, and on their way over to St. Martins Catholic Church on West Walnut Street. It took only ten minutes to get there. As they entered, Barton touched his finger in the Holy Water, crossed himself, held Ann Marie by the hand, and led her to pews about midway down the isle.

He knelt, motioned for Ann Marie to kneel beside him, handed her a small booklet with the Prayers of the Rosary, pointed to the place where the Reader was reading, smiled, and began repeating the Rosary. Ann Marie did the same.

The entire recital of the Rosary and the celebration of the

Mass lasted about an hour and ten minutes. Not one word was spoken between them. All communications had been in the form of a look, a gesture, a pointing of a finger.

Caught up in the spirit of the solemnity and the tranquility of the celebration of the Mass, Ann Marie sensed the oneness that she shared with Barton.

As they were leaving the Church, several members came to Ann Marie and congratulated her on her engagement; she, in turn, introduced them to Barton.

The Priest, at the entrance, bid his early bird parishioners a good morning, and shook hands with Barton and Ann Marie. "Welcome to Deer Hill and to St. Martin's"

"Thank you, Father."

Arm in arm, looking radiantly at peace with the Lord — and with themselves — they strolled the half block to Jane's Place.

They entered, were promptly seated at a marble-top table near a window facing out. They could see the beautiful Methodist Church with her inviting spires cascading in the sky.

"She seems to be ready for her flock."

Ann Marie grinned. "I have a lot of friends who attend church there; they do it at a decent hour of the day." In an afterthought, she added, "But, I did enjoy the early Mass at St. Martin's"

At a long marble top table near the back of the café, a group of men, having their morning coffee, were dropping steel balls down a circular spout onto a round board with carved holes big enough to hold the balls. Each hole had a numbered value assigned. Barton was intrigued.

He watched one man drop the three balls through the wire spigot, cross his fingers, watch intently, the balls circling on the round board. He counted aloud, "Fifty. Fifty. Twenty-five.

That's one hundred twenty five." He took his hat and walked out. His coffee would be paid for by the last and lowest scoring person.

The special of the morning was a Salt Fish Breakfast.

Ann Marie peered over her half-empty coffee cup, closed one eye. With the open eye, she looked at Barton, suggested the Salt Fish. He agreed, sipped coffee, continued to observe the men spinning the steel balls while at the same time trying to pay attention to what Ann Marie was telling him.

As the "ball-spinners" left Jane's Place, they waved to Barton and Ann Marie, but none stopped by their table.

The clerk brought the salt fish, eggs, stovetop cornbread and syrup.

They ate heartily, in silence, and washed their food down with their coffee.

Ann Marie finally broke the silence, "Will you explain the Mass to me?"

"In your church, do you ever celebrate, or rather, reenact the Last Supper?"

"Yes, usually at Easter time."

"Well, you too then, have celebrated the Mass. However, in the Catholic Church, the Mass is celebrated every time the doors are opened, and sometimes when they are not."

The clerk brought the ticket. While awaiting his change, he continued with his explanation of the Mass.

"The Mass is an action of Christ and of the Church, and it is the central act of worship on the part of Catholics. God speaks to you and you speak to him through your prayers, songs and responses. You offer yourself and your gifts to him; and, he offers himself to you through his priest in the form of a sacred banquet which is a distinct nourishment of the holy spirit."

"Then, almost all Christians, at one time or another, actually celebrate the Mass."

"That is true." Then he recited, "A rose by any other name is still a rose."

The clerk brought the change.

Barton left her a tip, thanked her for the breakfast, held the chair for Ann Marie to get up, took her by the elbow, left Jane's Place, retraced their steps to the car in front of St. Martin's Catholic Church, got in, started the engine, pulled away from the curb, and headed back to Ann Marie's house. He glanced at his watch. It was 9:30. Members of the various churches in the area were beginning to gather.

They turned the corner on to Cherry Street, now full of parked cars belonging to the folks attending the several churches.

Ann Marie, as if giving a guided tour, pointed to The Church Of Christ on the corner of Walnut and Cherry. The Presbyterian on the corner of Academy and Cherry. The First Baptist on the corner of College and Cherry.

Cherry Street is truly an Avenue of Churches.

He eased the Mercedes through the narrow street, turned left on College Street, also full of parked cars, slowed his car to a creep, as the space on the street was very limited. He finally reached Ann Marie's house. There, they encountered other parked cars belonging to the people attending the Episcopal Church on the corner of College and Pine. He thought to himself, "No one is at home. They are all in church, somewhere."

He stopped the Mercedes in the drive and got out to fetch the papers. Glancing at the headlines as he walked back to the car, Barton was jarred by the loud noise of a door slamming coming from the house of the widow Langur. He glanced toward the rear of the house and saw a man running toward the next street. He caught a glimpse of the fleeing man's face. "Is that Mr. Tom Bradleton?" he asked himself. He forgot the incident somewhere between parking the car in the garage and joining Ann Marie upstairs.

She was in the process of changing her Sunday clothes and was down to her bra and panties when he came into the bedroom.

He admired her, in awe of her beauty. A beauty from any angle. This view was from the back. He thought how lucky he was to have such a prize for a wife.

Memories came to him of his mother and father. On Sundays, they would go to Mass. Those were happy, happy times. Now, he was about to take a wife. His parents would be proud.

Until this moment, Ann Marie had been the aggressor in the love-making; but, now, in a nostalgic, amorous mood, he felt the urge to initiate the seduction of this fair maiden. He eased behind her, lifted her hair, kissed her neck, unsnapped her bra and let it fall to the floor. She remained standing, slightly quivering, yet trying not to appear too eager. But, when he reached around her chest and cupped her breast into his hands, her excitability aroused him to extreme rigidity. She reached back and gently caressed him. He moved his hands to her panties, slid them down her legs and finally to the floor. She stepped out of them just as he picked her up and laid her on the bed.

After the loving, they lay together. Ann Marie propped on one elbow, stroked the hair on his chest with the finger which held her engagement ring, and whispered, "My dearest husband to be. This 'intimate encounter' as Mary Louise would classify it, has brought me full circle with my beau, and I am, for the moment, completely satisfied."

Barton sat up, twirled her tangled hair, and responded ever so gently, "That oneness with us surely is what could make a baby."

"I hope so. We have gone through many Trojans, plus a couple of other times, and now, I am ready to tie the knot." She kissed him, asked him to explain the Rosary.

He sat up, pulling the sheet over his knees to hide his nakedness, crossed his arms and answered.

"The Rosary depicts the scenes from the life of Jesus and Mary. Or, you could say the events, or the mysteries, from the life of Jesus and Mary." He gathered his thoughts and continued, "In a way, by us meditating on these truths, we come to a better spiritual understanding of religion." He leaned over, kissed her on the forehead, gave her a loving gaze. "You were taught to believe in the Incarnation of the Lord, the Redemption, and the Christian life. These are the truths that I was taught. The Rosary is a prayerful sequence in which we meditate these mysteries."

"I recognized The Apostles' Creed. The Our Father. But, I could not grasp the Hail Mary."

"Let me explain it this way. The complete Rosary is composed of fifteen decades divided into three distinct parts containing five decades each." He got out of bed and fetched a pencil and paper and jumped back under the sheets. "Let me see if I can remember, and you help me as I try to write them down."

"Together, they started their catechisms. They listed the five Joyful Mysteries in the Life of Jesus and Mary, then the five Sorrowful Mysteries, and with little effort, the five Glorious Mysteries."

He was impressed with Ann Marie's knowledge of religion, and proceeded to tell her that the Hail Mary is said in groups of ten, to form one decade, while at the same time one of the Mysteries is being meditated.

"When we go back to Mass, I'll know how to pray the Rosary." She was still mumbling something as she crawled out of bed and went into the bathroom, content.

At 12:30, both Barton and Ann Marie were dressed. She wore a skirt, blouse and saddle oxfords, while he wore khaki pants, opened collar shirt and penny loafers.

Barton had emptied the several trash cans into one, carried it outside to the dump.

Judge and Mrs. Marbling came driving into the garage. He waved as he continued to empty the trash. Ann Marie was hugging her parents and showing them her ring when he returned.

As Barton got near, Mrs. Marbling met him with a big hug. "I knew that I liked you the first time that I heard your voice over the phone."

He whispered to her, "I think we have the matter of religion squared away."

Mrs. Marbling tip toed, kissed him on the check, returned in a whisper, "I didn't think that you would have any trouble with that."

Judge Marbling, walking arm in arm with Ann Marie, came to Barton, shook his hand, gave him that quizzical look of previous meetings. "Mr. Sandeau, it will be an honor to have you as a son." Then he released Barton's hand and hugged him tightly.

A tear came into Barton's eyes as he remembered his father hugging him.

All four stood motionless, embraced for a few seconds, then Ann Marie spoke to her Mother.

"Barton and I want to get married, and I mean as soon as possible. Say like right now."

Mrs. Marbling laughed joyfully and responded, "You must at least have a marriage license."

"Daddy can take care of that, can't he?"

Judge Marbling answered, "We will have to wait, at least, until the court house is open in the morning."

They entered the main house through the screened portico when Ann Marie stopped. She announced: "Barton and I are flying to his hometown this afternoon so that he can take care of some business tomorrow. And, we'll either fly back Monday evening or early Tuesday morning."

"But you two are not married yet."

Mrs. Marbling looked at her husband, remarked, "And neither were we when we spent a weekend at your house where your parents were conveniently absent."

He grinned his approval. "What difference does it make? Here or in Bessemer."

CHAPTER 14

Ebb and Flossie

Ann Marie asked her mother to join her upstairs while she packed an overnight bag. When they reached her room, she hugged her mother and inquired, "Does daddy still love you as much as he did when you got married?"

"Why of course." She hesitated and then remarked, "This weekend was almost like our honeymoon all over again." She winked at her daughter.

"Good. Then I have a lot to look forward to, with Barton." She smiled, confirming what her mother had already guessed: "Ann Marie knows man."

She quickly finished her bag and asked her mother, "Any parting, good advice, to a young lady who is about to go home with her fiancé?"

Mrs. Marbling laughed, "No. As an adult, you are responsible for your own acts." Then she hugged her.

"Thanks. But, can't I call on you from time to time?"

Mrs. Marbling smiled. "Anytime."

They descended the stairs and found Judge Marbling and Barton discussing flying. Barton already had his small bag and was eager to get started. He took Ann Marie's bag, said goodbye to Judge and Mrs. Marbling and headed for the car.

Mrs. Wards was still in her office at the airport when they

arrived. She reported that the Stinson had not yet returned as scheduled, but the 150 was available.

"Why not. It's been awhile since I flew one of those."

He finished the paperwork and then did his pre-flight on the ramp. His assigned time of departure was 2:45 Central or 7:45 Zulu.

The flight, in the 150 to Bessemer, took an hour and a half; and another twenty minutes to land due to the heavy Sunday afternoon traffic of private pilots, either practicing or continuing with the flying lessons.

Bessemer Airport did not have a control tower; but, the Unicom was blaring with young pilots trying to get a position to land or else a position sequence to take off.

Finally, Barton eased the 150 into a sequence in the downwind, precisely parallel to 4th Avenue. He was behind a Gruman: kept appropriate spacing; so the landing would be in an orderly manner on this very busy single airstrip.

He glanced down, just before he turned base leg to the approach, observed that there were as many airplanes in the sky as there were cars on US 11, aka 4th Avenue. On base leg, still trailing the Gruman, he notched ten degrees of flaps, eased back on the throttle, glided to the point where he turned final, knew that he was cleared as the Gruman was already on the runway and turning at the middle intersection He notched ten more degrees, cut the engine to idle, eased the trim tab back, set her down on the numbers, applied a little brake, turned on the first intersection, moved aside to let a departing plane taxi, followed the attendants signal to the parking ramp, secured the plane, got out, helped Ann Marie tie the 150 to the chocks, grabbed their bags, locked the doors, gave the attendant the service order, and stated, "I would like to leave her overnight."

With the two overnight bags in each hand he walked over to the operations office, and waited for Ann Marie to return from the rest room. He spotted a cab out front, rushed out, asked the driver if he could wait, that he had one in the john.

The cab driver laughed and motioned with his head that he would wait.

Seated in the cab, Barton gave the Clarendon Avenue address to the driver who was listening to a baseball broadcast between the Birmingham Barons and the Atlanta Crackers.

The driver again acknowledged with a nod, drove out of the fenced area of the airport, onto US 11 (4th Avenue) turned right on Central Avenue, drove to Jonesboro, turned left, made his way to Clarendon, through the railroad tunnel and on to Barton's house.

They left the cab and walked the few steps to the porch, unlocking the door. They stepped inside, switched on a light in the living room and moved on to a small hall separating two bedrooms, each with its own bath. They went to the bedroom toward the back of the house and put the overnight bags on the bed. He took Ann Marie's hand, led her back into the hall, through the dining room, through the kitchen, and onto the screened sleeping porch that spanned the entire rear of the house, and with steep steps leading to the yard of the gently sloped lot.

"See that white house? That's Ebb and Flossie's house, long-time employees of the family. And that," he said, pointing at another building, "is the garage. That back half of the lot is Ebb's garden."

It was almost 6 P.M. Barton knew that Ebb and Flossie would probably be at their church. They always attended every third Sunday where the congregation gathered for an all-day singing and dinner on the ground. And, continuing with the practices of his father, Ebb would probably be driving the '39 Chevrolet Sedan.

They were still standing looking out from the sleeping porch when he asked Ann Marie, "Are you hungry? You know, we never did get any lunch."

"I sure am. But don't count on any food here. When we came through the kitchen, I noticed that the refrigerator door was open, clean as a whistle, and the power chord was laying across the top."

"We'll have to catch a cab. But, first let me see if we can get a place for us to eat." He picked up the phone, asked the operator to ring the Bright Star Café. "We're in luck," he said, the phone nestled in the crook of his shoulder and ear, "the Bright Star Café can handle the reservation for two if we don't mind being seated near the server's booth."

He accepted the reservations, pushed the phone lever down, released it and asked the operator to ring him the Checker Cab Company.

He looked at Ann Marie. "All set for 6:30."

She went into the bathroom to freshen up. Barton went to his closet and chose a blue blazer, shook it, put it on.

The horn tooted. It was the cab. They made their way out of the house and to the cab at the curb, boarded, and sat quietly as the driver took them to the Bright Star Café. They glanced at the old town as they got out, then went in.

As they entered, Jimmy, one of the owners, flirted as he gave Ann Marie an approving look, remarking to Barton, "We have upgraded your table only because you grace our premises with this gorgeous lady."

"You are a prince Jimmy. This is my fiancée, Ann Marie Marbling."

Upon hearing "fiancée," several of the folks nearby who knew

Barton, waved an expression of recognition.

The meal of veal, fried green tomatoes, raison and carrot salad, pickled beets, corn sticks, ice tea, and lemon coconut pie was just about consumed when Monsignor Durrinack, and his entourage of Priests, and affluent parishioners of St. Aloysius Catholic Church, stopped at Barton's table.

Barton stood, shook the Monsignor's hand, expressed happiness in seeing him. He shook hands with all of the others including Mr. Schiller, then asked them to meet his fiancée, Ann Marie Marbling.

After the greetings, he asked Monsignor if he could have an audience with him tomorrow.

"I'll be returning to Mobile early tomorrow. What is it that I can do for you, my young friend?"

"Monsignor, Ann Marie and I are to be married soon, and we need a special dispensation to be married on the altar of St. Martin's in Deer Hill."

Monsignor Durrinack looked at one of his prelates and directed, "Make a note for me to write Father Stillmac granting Barton's request." He hesitated a moment and added, "The rectory there is not adequate for a wedding."

The Priest wrote as the Monsignor had instructed, then added a comment of his own.

"Your excellency, one as pretty as Miss Marbling deserves the full exposure of our church."

Uncertain that she should speak in the presence of such hierarchy of the Catholic Church, Ann Marie, having a mind of her own, replied, "Thank you Father." She smiled at the Monsignor. "And thank you, Monsignor Durrinack. In time, I imagine that we will have a lot of little Catholics running around Deer Hill."

Mr. Schiller leaned across Barton and kissed Ann Marie on the cheek. When he straightened up, he told Barton, "You have a jewel here."

Monsignor Durrinack spoke, "Barton, it is good to see you. If you can find time, drop by and see mama. Seeing you will make her day."

"Thank you Monsignor, I will take Ann Marie to see her tomorrow, maybe take her to lunch."

He shook hands with each of the Monsignor's party, bid to each a good evening, sat down beside Ann Marie and explained, "I visited in the home of the parents of the Monsignor, and I played with his brothers." He stood up, motioned for the waiter to bring the ticket.

Jimmy came over instead. "Mr. Schiller paid your tab and the tip."

He shook Jimmy's hand, thanked him again for the upgrade, and the fine food, then he and Ann Marie walked out onto the sidewalk just as a trolley was passing by.

"Have you ever ridden a streetcar?"

"No. I have never even seen one except in the picture show, and just now."

"Good. Let's catch one and ride. It runs two blocks from the house so we can walk a little of our supper off."

They stepped down off the streetcar and slowly walked arm in arm toward the house, discussing, without a care in the world, that which needed to be done tomorrow.

It was almost nine o'clock when Barton put the key into the front door lock and turned it to open. Once inside, he asked Ann Marie, "You about ready to hit the sack?"

"Yep. But, I don't want to go to sleep just yet." He took her hand and led her into the bedroom.

The next morning, he was awakened by a familiar shuffle in the kitchen. He rolled over, glanced at his watch, noted the time to be 7:30, stretched as if he had just gone to sleep, eased out of the bed so not to disturb Ann Marie, who was sleeping soundly, slipped on his trousers, and walked barefooted into the kitchen.

He already knew who it was shuffling in the kitchen, so he eased up behind Flossie and kissed her neck.

"You do that one more time and that cute thing in that bed in there will have some sho'nuff competition." Then she laughed, hugged him around the shoulder, leaned back, gave him a motherly look and asked, "You two married?"

Before Barton could answer, Ann Marie entered, clad only in Barton's long-sleeve shirt and remarked, "You don't buy something that you haven't tried." She hugged Flossie, flashed her diamond ring, stating, "We are going to be married at Mass next Saturday in St. Martin's Catholic Church in Deer Hill. And, I would be honored and proud if you and Ebb could be there."

"No way that Ebb and me could make it that far." Flossie gave a slight frown. She knew that she had to be there but didn't want to make a promise that she might not be able to keep. She turned her head slightly aside and mumbled, "Ebb and I got to look after things here."

She recovered from the feeling that she and Ebb might be put out if the property was sold; patted Ann Marie on the rump and said, "We'll be thinking about you, and probably the next time I see you, this thing will be big as mine."

Ann Marie jokingly laughed, "So, what!" She said, leaving the kitchen, and proceeded to get dressed for the day.

Barton looked at Flossie and humbly asked, "Are you jealous?"

"Maybe a little. But, I know we got to give you up sometime.

And, she sho' is a mighty fine young lady. And, I sho' do like her."

He went back to his room, put on the shirt that Ann Marie had taken off, slipped on his socks and loafers, returned to the kitchen to visit with Flossie while she was preparing breakfast. He thought about Mrs. Durrinack, went to the phone, gave her a call.

She had other plans for the day, but would take a rain check. He visited briefly with her, then bid her a good day, hung up the phone just as Ann Marie entered looking great in her multi-colored blouse, solid navy blue skirt, white tennis shoes that somehow accentuated the calves in her legs as she walked softly in front of her fiancé.

CHAPTER 15

Girl Talk

Flossie heard Ebb coming up the back steps; she took a couple of steps toward the bedrooms and yelled, "Breakfast is ready. Come and get it!"

Barton hurried through the kitchen and on to the sleeping porch, hugged Ebb, thanked him for taking care of everything while he was gone, then returned with him to the kitchen where he introduced him to Ann Marie. He held a chair for Ann Marie, as did Ebb for Flossie.

When all four were seated, Ebb asked that they bow their heads.

"Bless us, O Lord, and these your gifts, which we are about to receive from your bounty, through Christ, Our Lord. Amen," softly recited Ebb who had learned this Prayer Of Grace from Barton when he was a young boy.

The four sat at the small round table in the kitchen enjoying their meal of country ham, grits, red-eye gravey, eggs, and Flossie's very special biscuits. Ebb finished his breakfast and began telling Barton about the real estate man.

"He brought this couple to see us and we showed them the house. They want to engage Flossie, and if possible, they would like to also lease the car with me as the driver. They can't drive." Ebb took a final sip of his coffee and added, "The real estate man told him what you said about the part of the property that they could lease."

He paused a moment, a little apprehensive, yet confident, and continued, "The real estate man took him to the sleeping porch, pointed out the part that he could lease. We told him it would be from the front street to the upper side of the garden." Again, he paused and asked, "Is the rest of it still to be used by me and Flossie as always with Miss Hester and Mr. Mathew?"

Barton stood, putting his hand on Ebb's shoulder. "If it suits you. And, if you think that you will like that arrangement with the new tenants, then I am all for it. And, yes, the rest will be used by you and Flossie as always with Mama and Daddy."

Flossie spoke, "I do believe that we will get along fine. All she asked for when she moves in, is that we have the cabinets, pantry and closets empty. She wants us to take the silver, china and crystal out of the house. She don't want to be responsible for it. And she has her own." She winked at Ann Marie. "And the pay is pretty good."

Barton asked, "What about the storage under the sleeping porch?"

Ebb replied, "They said that there was room there for our stuff and theirs so that wouldn't be a problem."

"Well, if you and Flossie are satisfied, while I am downtown, I will go by the real estate office and sign the lease." He turned to Ann Marie and asked if she would like to go with him downtown while he went by the bank, real estate office, and a few other errands that he needed to run.

"I believe that I will stay here and help Flossie get the house ready for the new tenants."

"Okay. If you will pack the china and crystal, we will take it to Deer Hill with us." In the next breath, he told Flossie and

Ebb to take the stuff in the pantry.

He kissed Ann Marie on the cheek, then Flossie, and announced that he should not be gone more than a couple of hours.

Ebb left for the garden. Ann Marie and Flossie finished with the breakfast dishes and began to pack. As each piece of china was dried, Flossie would wrap it in newspaper that she had saved, then place it in the boxes that Ebb had brought her. She packed the crystal the same way. They went to the China Cabinet, brought the other four place settings, and packed them. In all, there were four boxes, and the cedar silver case, that would go to Deer Hill.

They next packed the contents of the pantry which consisted mostly of canned goods. Flossie called to Ebb to come and move these to their house.

They put clean linens on the beds, dusted the furniture, and by noon, the entire house was spotless and smelled fresh as Flossie had opened the windows about four inches and turned on the attic fan. This draft coming through the four-inch opening, in the windows caused the fresh air and the lace curtains to flow inward.

And, during the course of all this cleaning, Ann Marie asked Flossie to tell her about Aunt Alva.

As they dusted or whatever, Flossie, with an occasional pause to emphasize a certain point, told to Ann Marie, the story as she understood it.

"Miss Alva and Miss Hester, by the providence of God, showed up at the hospital on the same day and within a few minutes of each other. They birthed their babies — both boys. Miss Alva went into some kind of trance like a voodoo spell had come over her.

"She wouldn't let the baby nurse, so Miss Hester told them to bring the baby to her that she had enough milk for the both of them. Well, the doctor, and Miss Alva's mother, thought maybe they needed to leave the baby alone with Miss Alva for a few minutes. Maybe that would bring her out of her trance." She paused a moment as a tear fell on her cheek, continued with a choking sound, "It was awful. It seems, somehow, in all the commotion of Miss Hester feeding both babies, and the hospital nursery being crowded, and the doctor being real busy, they left the baby with Miss Alva for over two hours. Then, two of the nurses got into an argument over which baby had been taken to Miss Alva. What they found in the room when they went in was not very pretty. The baby had been smothered."

"How awful." Cried Ann Marie who asked, "And, they were never sure which baby was which?"

"Never. And that's when all that insane hearing took place, and Miss Alva was sent to that hospital in Tuscaloosa."

"What about Miss Hester?"

"Oh, she mourned, but she was a strong person and just said, 'well, we'll never know, and I don't think that I want to know' and that was the last time it was brought up about the babies being switched."

"You can be sure that it makes no difference to me. My Barton will never be confronted by me on the subject. I love that man, Flossie."

"I know you do, honey. When I saw that gold ring with that birthstone and diamonds on your right had, I figured that you had done dropped your pants."

"You bet. I dropped them, and may never put them back on."

They were both laughing aloud when Barton came into the room. "What are you laughing so hard about?" he asked as they giggled.

Ann Marie answered, "We'll never tell."

"All right, keep your secrets." Then he told them that he had noticed Sam, at the house at the end of the alley, was fixing his famous fish sandwiches and suggested that he fetch some of them for lunch.

Flossie stated, "He sho does cook that fish mighty good. I heard that he had been fishing and caught a mess and that he would be cooking today."

"I'll fix some ice tea, but we'll have to get glasses and ice from my house as we done packed all that crystal, and I done cleaned the ice box several days ago."

Barton passed Ebb, still working his garden. "How many of Sam's fish sandwiches can you eat?" he asked. Ebb held up two fingers and kept working. Barton kept walking toward the alley and over to Sam's place.

While he was gone, Flossie made the tea, and told Ann Marie about Miss Hester and Mr. Mathew.

"Miss Hester had been flying those airplanes a long time before the war broke out, and she would fly them things to wherever. That's when Mr. Mathew and Ebb would take Barton on fishing trips over on the river. Then when Miss Hester would come back, we would all have a big fish fry in the back yard.

"Then Mr. Mathew got drafted."

"Did Miss Hester keep ferrying the planes?"

"Oh, yeah, she started taking them across the water. She would be gone about ten days each time. While she was gone, Ebb and I would sleep up here. If it was warm enough, all three of us would sleep on the porch. Then, when Miss Hester would come back, Ebb would drive us all over to the Birmingham airport and pick her up. It was while she was home that she started teaching Barton to fly those airplanes."

Tears began to fall on Flossie's cheek as she slowly continued. "Then when she was on one of her flying trips, that awful telegram came that says we regret to inform you and so on. That's when Ebb went to the YMCA and fetched Barton and brought him home, then we all read the telegram. Ebb, in all of our sorrow, forgot that Miss Hester was supposed to arrive at the airport at noon. And when she phoned, it was all I could do to keep a cheerful voice until we could be with her. Ebb got the car out, but thought it would be a good idea to let Barton drive. He was only fifteen, but he was a good little driver. I sat in the back and prayed. Miss Hester was having her lunch at the airport grill when we found her. Barton went to her and during their embrace, told her that his daddy had been killed in the line of duty, then he handed her the telegram."

"What did Miss Hester do?" Ann Marie humbly inquired.

"Well, honey, she put her hands on Barton's shoulders, told him that she lived in fear of getting that telegram. She took from her purse that ring you're wearing, put it on his finger and told him that he was the only other man that she would ever love."

"I need to give it back to him."

"No. Not, just yet." Flossie scolded, "You keep that ring on your finger until you gets before that preacher and says I do."

Ann Marie hugged Flossie and asked in a most humble and sympathetic tone, "Did Miss Hester keep on flying?"

"Even more so, instead of one flight per month, she would do two, and finally, she would come home only about every other month. She seemed to survive on her flying since she lost Mr. Mathew.

"What did Barton do?" chirped Ann Marie.

"Well, he was sixteen soon after that telegram came. Mr. Red brought that 1933 Plymouth to the house. He said that Miss

Hester had bought it for Barton's sixteenth birthday," proudly announced Flossie.

"How did he manage?"

"Oh, we did fine. He slept up here but ate with me and Ebb, or at times, we would cook up here. He was in his last year of high school, when that other telegram came. It seems that Miss Hester's plane went down somewhere near a place called Newfoundland."

"How did Barton pay you and Ebb for looking after him?"

"Oh, honey! Its the other way round. That ring and that car was not all that Mr. Barton got. He got the insurance money, this house and some other things. And he told me and Ebb that we could continue living in our house without ever paying any rent. So you see, we are more than paid for what we do for your man."

Ann Marie moved to Flossie, hugged her."You did a good job. I hope that I can equal it when I'm his wife."

"Honey, with your equipment, you can keep him happy for the rest of his life."

They both burst out laughing. And, were still laughing when Barton and Ebb came in with the fish sandwiches.

"You two have been giggling all morning," he said mildly, as he handed the fish sandwiches to each of them.

CHAPTER 16

The Inquest

The fish sandwiches were devoured while sitting on the cool sleeping porch, and pretty much in silence, as everyone appeared hungry, and possibly a little tired.

Flossie became a little nostalgic as she hated to see Barton go, but she knew she should not express such feelings. She and Ebb had become attached to him. Finally, she broke the silence and told Ebb that it was time for the little birds to leave their nest.

Barton smiled, hugged her, and chirped like a bird, "Just because Ann Marie is coming into our family is no reason for you to be jealous. You'll have two of us to love now, and who knows, you may have more in the near future."

"Oh! I'm not jealous of Ann Marie. It's just that I'm gonna miss you being round and miss doing the little things for you 'cause I know all of us have been so lonesome since our family was gobbled up by that awful war." Tears streamed down her cheek.

Ebb took her into his arms. "Honey, we've been blessed in having Barton since we don't have any of our own, and what's to keep us from keeping him even though he will be in another town."

Ann Marie's tears were falling on her beautiful face. She wiped them.

"Miss Flossie and Mr. Ebb. You two will see a lot of us, I promise."

Barton spoke, "That's true, and now before I start crying, Ebb you had best take us to the airport."

"Whenever you're ready."

Flossie and Ann Marie each carried a box of the china to the 1939 Sedan parked in the garage. Ebb had carried the chest of silver, and Barton had carried his clothes that he had not stored in the cedar bureau in the basement under the porch.

In no time, Ebb had maneuvered the car out of the alley and on its way to the Bessemer airport on 4th Avenue. Upon reaching the airport, Ebb easily found a parking space as the traffic on Monday was nothing like it was yesterday. Everybody carried a box to the airplane where Barton carefully placed them in the small baggage compartment, in accordance with the weight-and-balance arrangement that he had computed. He placed the silver chest under the front seat and latched it down so it would not slide. He stacked two of the boxes on top of the other two and secured them with the baggage straps. He hung his clothes on top of them.

He had figured that Ann Marie's weight plus the weight of the silver chest would not overload the front seats

Once the airplane was loaded, Flossie told them that she had to get Ebb ready for work as he worked the three-to-eleven shift at the mill.

Barton gave a quick glance at his watch and realized that Ebb really needed to go; but he also knew that Flossie did not want to see them takeoff. She had not liked airplanes since Miss Hester's death.

Pre flight completed, Barton went inside the small operations office, filed a VFR Flight Plan, since the weather was clear all over the southeast, and he wanted to give Ann Marie an opportunity to operate the controls of the airplane. He paid for his gas and overnight tie down, returned to the airplane, once again gave her a look around. He handed Ann Marie the checklist, and proceeded to prepare for takeoff.

At 2 P.M., the 150 lifted off the runway and rotated into the beautiful, bright, blue sky.

He had the 150 trimmed and flying smoothly; and, he was feeling good that he had done all the chores that he needed to do in Bessemer, and was now enroute to Deer Hill where he could get things in order for his marriage to Ann Marie on the upcoming Saturday which will be five days away.

He reached over and began to flirt with Ann Marie.

"Go slow, lover, the play pretty is out of commission and will be for the next six days."

Barton laughed, "What timing," he thought.

He had heard about the menstrual cycle of females, and now, was experiencing the opportunity to carry out the suggestions of Dr. Ragsdale. "It must be nice to clear your system periodically." He paused. "I guess that we are not pregnant." He paused again and stated, "Yet."

Ann Marie chuckled. "No, but we certainly will get to that once we are married and on our own." Then she added, "Flossie and I were giggling about several things. One was that I borrowed a Kotex from her. It was a large, so we got the scissors and trimmed it. When you came in, she had just told me to give it time, and it would not need to be trimmed."

Barton broke out in an achieving laugh just about the time that Montgomery Radio ask him his position. He readily got a cross fix on Selma and Montgomery, reported five miles north on radial 308.

The visibility, as far as the naked eye could see, enabled him to see Deer Hill, as he turned on course from the Montgomery VOR. He picked up the skyline of the City of Deer Hill, and shortly after that, he was able to see the airport environment. He reported to Montgomery that he had a visual of the Deer Hill airport and asked them to cancel his flight plan. He called Deer Hill Unicom and was told runway 14 was the active, and no other reported traffic. He put the mike back on its rack, made a slight course correction, did his pre landing check, adjusted all systems, announced straight in approach to the landing on runway 14, turned at the intersection and taxied to the gas pumps.

Judge and Mrs. Marbling, who Ann Marie had called before leaving the house on Clarendon, were waiting near the hangar with the Chief of Police. All three walked out toward the plane. Barton had gotten out and gone around to help Ann Marie. She was already on the ground headed for her parents. He joined her.

Judge Marbling spoke, "Barton, the Chief here, seems to think that you may have been a witness to Clarabelle Bradleton's accident on Thursday, and he would like for you to attend the inquest this afternoon at 4:30." Barton looked at his watch. It was 3:30. He asked, "Let me get these things to the Inn, and I'll go straight to the City Hall."

Mrs. Marbling chimed, "Ann Marie and I have talked. And, if okay with you, we want you to move into the garage apartment, and when you are married, you may live there if you so choose." He hugged her, announced that he would get the car, gave Ann Marie his wallet and a note with the tachometer time on it, asked her to settle the account with Mrs. Wards, and then went to the parking lot.

He drove the car to the ramp, parked a safe distance from the airplane, transferred, with the help of the Judge, Mrs. Marbling, Ann Marie, and even the Chief, the cargo of the plane to the car.

Ann Marie took the box from each of the bearers and placed it carefully in the trunk and scotched them so that they would not shift, then she hung Barton's clothes on the rack in the back seat.

She drove the loaded car behind her parents to their home and the garage apartment where all four of them unloaded the goods and took them upstairs.

It was 4:10, and Barton asked how to get to the City Hall. With the directions, he kissed Ann Marie, went with the Judge, who took him to the Inn to get his car.

Since he had only ten minutes to make the inquest, he got out of the Judge's car and into his and drove over to Elm Street, to the dead end where the Police Station and the City Court was located.

He went inside the court room. It was a small room furnished with a small table, three chairs, a chalkboard on one wall, and eight benches without back supports.

He sat down on the back bench, waved to the Chief who was standing near the City Judge, and two other men, who turned out to be the Coroner, and the City Attorney, and a clerk who must have been the recorder.

Mr. Tom Bradleton and his attorney sat on the first bench at the extreme left side.

Mrs. Maudie Jefferson, her husband, and several other ladies sat on the second bench at the extreme right side.

Barton mused silently, "At least the gladiators are somewhat separated."

The remaining benches were partially filled with other people scattered about and were either curiosity seekers, or perhaps witnesses.

The Coroner rapped gently on the table. "This inquest is now open and the Robert's Rules of Order will prevail; therefore the meeting will now come to order, and the Autopsy Report of Mrs. Clarabelle Bradleton will now be given."

A man with spectacles stood in one corner where he could face the three at the table, and also be seen by the people seated on the benches, and began, "This autopsy of the deceased, Clarabelle Thompson Bradleton, was performed by the Department of Forensic Sciences in accordance with the legal procedures outlined for such autopsies." He flipped the page and continued reading, "The findings of this autopsy is that the deceased, Clarabelle Thompson Bradleton, died of a severe blow to the head, and these findings places the time of death to be between 10:30 A.M. and 11:30 on Thursday, the 17th day of April, 1948."

He paused a moment and looked at the City Judge and confirmed, "All appropriate signatures are affixed." Then he handed the document to the clerk.

It took a moment for the autopsy report information to soak in, then Barton thought to himself. The time frame of the death is different from the time that the Green Cadillac tried to pass him. Maybe Mrs. Maudie Jefferson is justified in asking for the inquest.

His thoughts were interrupted by the City Judge who spoke, "We now have the autopsy report duly recorded. Our next order of business will be to hear witnesses."

He turned to Mrs. Maudie Jefferson, asked if she would like to call any witnesses who could shed any light on the cause of death of her sister, Clarabelle Thompson Bradleton.

Mrs. Maudie Jefferson called Mrs. Myrtle Overale, a back-yard neighbor of the Tom Bradletons.

Mrs. Myrtle Overale stood and answered the inquiry by saying, "Yes, I am Myrtle Overale. I do live in Deer Hill. I did know Clarabelle Bradleton. And, I am here to say that I believe that there was hanky panky in her death, and that her no-good husband was at the bottom of it."

The City Judge rapped the table and disgustingly retorted, "Mrs. Overale, we are not here to state what we believe or to express ill will toward anyone. If you do not have any facts, and I mean concrete facts, surrounding the death of Clarabelle Thompson Bradleton, then please sit down." Then he asked, "Do you have any material facts which would lend any credence to this inquest?"

"No," she said, curtly. Then to get another shot at Tom Bradleton, she said quickly, "He treated her awful."

The City Judge looked sternly at her, "Mrs. Overale, you are out of order." He turned to Mrs. Maudie Jefferson. "Do you have other witnesses who have information regarding Clarabelle's death?"

"Yes. I would like to call Mr. Barton Sandeau." She spoke as she pointed toward Barton.

Barton crawled over Judge Marbling, who had eased in beside him, walked down the side of the room to the front near the table.

The City Judge asked, "Mr. Sandeau, what do you know about the death of Clarabelle Thompson Bradleton?"

"Sir. I know nothing. In fact, I am appalled to have been called to this inquest," he said in a matter-of-fact manner.

"Mrs. Maudie Jefferson, in a rage, jumped up, shouted, "He's done bought you off, too, you bastard child of Jarvis Bydian."

The City Judge rapped the gavel.

Undisturbed by the ranting of Miss Maudie Jefferson, Barton

maintained his nonchalant manner, shrugging his shoulders. The Judge asked, "Mr. Sandeau, do you wish to say anything else.?"

"Your Honor, if is in order, I would like a moment, in private, with Mrs. Maudie Jefferson, perhaps in the Police Chief's office."

The City Judge looked at Mrs. Jefferson, asked, "Would you like to talk with him in private?"

She did not speak as she stood and walked the short distance to the Chief's office, where she was met by Barton who had advised the City Judge that it would only take a second.

Alone with Mrs. Maudie Jefferson in the Chief's Office with the adjoining door not fully closed, Barton spoke in a very low tone. "Mrs. Jefferson, one, I know nothing about the death of your sister. Two, I have not been bought off. And, three, if you don't go back in there and apologize to me for your blatant conduct, I am going to reveal, right out there, in that room, what I saw and heard in the room adjacent to mine at the Deer Hill Inn, on Friday morning about 9 o'clock."

She stared daggers at him. Her face began to frown. Her eyes wallowed.

After a second, she walked back into the Court Room, half choking, told the City Judge that she wanted to apologize to the members of this hearing, and especially to Mr. Sandeau. She gave a whimper, motioned for her husband, and literally stomped out of the building.

The City Judge told Barton that he was free to leave that the inquest board was satisfied that he knew nothing about the death of Clarabelle Thompson Bradleton.

He thanked the City Judge, gave the Police Chief an abbreviated departing wave, walked to the rear of the room, joined

Judge Marbling who was now standing.

The Judge put his arm around his shoulder and said, "Let's go home to two beautiful women."

Barton gave an approving smile. "I need to go by the Inn, get my gear, and check out."

"Why don't I go with you and help. We might even have a cold beer in the lounge."

Sylvester spotted them as they were getting out of their cars and was opening the door for Judge Marbling when Barton came over and shook his hand, told him that he was checking out.

"Too late. Miss Ann Marie and Miss Mary Margaret done come and got your things. I checked to make sure that they did not leave anything." He grinned, then added, "Miss Ann Marie said for you to pay the bill, that she did not have that much money."

The Judge shook his head, laughing. "Let's get that beer, anyway."

"Sure thing. If you'll order the beer, I'll pay my bill, and then together we'll face two beautiful girls."

The two friends sat at a table in the lounge silently sipping their beers out of frozen mugs when Mrs. Marbling and Ann Marie walked in.

Mrs. Marbling spoke, "We heard over the radio what happened at the inquest. It made us so mad that we decided to find you."

Ann Marie was already sitting in Barton's lap with her head under his chin. She was crying and muttering, "They're not going to hurt you with their filthy mouths."

Barton patted her on the head, moved her head back and kissed her. "Hey, my gal don't cry over the likes of what took place at the inquest. Besides, a lady in your condition needs a beer."

Mrs. Marbling's eyes brightened. "Better get me a beer too, as I don't know what condition our condition is in."

Ann Marie started laughing, leaned over and whispered into her Mother's ear.

CHAPTER 17

Special Dispensation

Mrs. Marbling, responding to Ann Marie's whisper, also began to laugh, then noticing the quizzical look on the Judge's face, leaned over, whispered to him that Ann Marie's condition was merely that her menstrual period had started.

The Judge stood up laughing and announced, "That calls for a celebration." He sat down and called for another round of beer with cold mugs.

The four sat at the tiny table enjoying their cold beer and small talk when it dawned on the Judge that he had not given the marriage license to Barton. He reached into his jacket pocket, pulled out the fresh marriage license and spoke, "Mr. Barton Sandeau, I hereby, for the sum of one dollar and fifty cents American, present you with title to my beloved daughter to be your slave now and forever."

Ann Marie paid her father, saying, "My father, my dearest father, my dearest beloved generous father, I hereby now pay my indenture, and make to my beloved a gift of this title, and do hereby declare such title as being free of bondage."

They all laughed, then Barton asked, "Would you two be the guest of honor for dinner tonight? My beautiful orator will do the cooking."

Ann Marie looked surprised at Barton. Even though she had

learned to cook, and was considered a good cook, she did not know that he knew.

He grinned and said, "In the dining room of the Inn."

Judge Marbling was holding his wife's hand under the table as he leaned over and spoke, "Let's do have dinner here but Mary Margaret and I will 'cook'. As I expect that you two will need your money."

"Judge, you have been most kind to me, and I love you and Mrs. Marbling, but Ann Marie and I are not necessarily paupers." He brought forth a certified check from his pocket and held it so the Judge could see it.

Judge Marbling, with Mrs. Marbling's hand still in his, stood up, kissed his wife on the forehead, helped her to get up, and remarked, "My dear. We are the guest of this handsome young couple; shall we adjourn to the dining room?"

As they were leaving the lounge for the dining room, they met Father Stillmac who had entered the lobby through the side door next to the bar.

Barton hailed to him and invited him to join them for dinner.

Father Stillmac said, "I was about to have dinner myself, and I am glad that I ran into you."

Sam, the clerk who had served the Salt Fish breakfast, had observed the fivesome in the lobby and was waiting for them when they entered the dining room.

He took them to a round table near the center of the dining room, assisted them with their chairs, and asked if anyone would like a cocktail before dinner.

Judge and Mrs. Marbling ordered Martinis. Father Stillmac ordered red wine.

Barton became a little nostalgic as he recalled his parents drinking their Martinis and fixing him a Shirley Temple. He looked at Ann Marie. "Shirley Temple?"

Her parents laughed. But Ann Marie took his chin in her hand, and with a very solemn expression replied, "No, my love I will have another beer in a cold mug."

"Same for me."

While Sam went for the cocktails, Father Stillmac told Barton that he had received a call from Mobile, and that a special dispensation has been granted for the marriage to take place on the altar this coming Saturday at ten o'clock. Then he asked, "How do you know the Bishop, and the Monsignor?"

Ann Marie spoke up, "He played with his brothers in the house of the mother of the Monsignor. And I met him last Sunday night at the Bright Star Café in Bessemer."

Father Stillmac replied, "I know. He told me that you promised a lot of little Catholics."

Barton grinned.

Judge Marbling took the menu from Sam and suggested the food for the evening. Everyone agreed as they toasted the betrothed at their table.

Father Stillmac asked Ann Marie if there was any special scripture that she wanted for her wedding.

"We'll take the regular," she politely answered, "we just want to be married in the eyes of God, and all others who might venture to attend."

The conversation turned to minor points of wedding etiquette, with Mrs. Marbling asking about the flowers, decorations, music.

"What about guests?" Judge Marbling asked.

"Invite whoever you want. The Church is small, but all of my golfing parishioners usually go to the 7 o'clock Mass, but since almost all of them have already met Barton, I expect that many of them will attend the wedding."

Father Stillmac put into his mouth the last bite of his prime rib, and was chewing as he asked Ann Marie, "We can go over the usual wedding procedures now, if you like."

Ann Marie put a bite into her mouth and began to answer the Padré in a mimic manner when a commotion occurred in the wide French doors of the entrance to the dining room.

With both hands propped on her cane, her legs rigid as poles forming a tripod, Ole Miss Bydian appeared to be in a state of shock and staring at the five-some at the center table.

Sam, who had begun clearing the table, looked toward Ole Miss Bydian and remarked, "I believe the old devil has pissed in the floor." He thought about what he had said and looked at Mrs. Marbling, canted, "I'm sorry ma'am."

Ann Marie had puckered her jaws and lips to keep from laughing aloud, but Judge Marbling grinned and remarked, "Paul believes that his mother has gone entirely insane over the matter of a grandson."

Barton, who had finished his dinner but had hardly touched his beer, spoke in a gentle tone, "It is a pity that a person goes into their waning years trying to clear their conscience of deeds or misdeeds of their past." He paused, then stated in a matter-of-fact voice, "It would do her more good if she went to confession."

Paul and Betty Bydian, with their embarrassed daughter, Sara Lou, were coaxing the stunned lady out of the lobby, and things in the dining room were returning to normal, and Sam was attempting to serve dessert when Ann Marie asked, "Tell me about Confession."

Sam sat the dessert down and with an air of complete confidence. "I'll handle that one, Father," he said.

Then like a third grader reciting a poem, Sam stated, "Confession, or the Sacrament of Reconciliation, is where we receive God's healing forgiveness for sins committed after Baptism." And, with a great deal of satisfaction, Sam accepted the approving expression of Father Stillmac, and then served the dessert.

Ann Marie chimed, "In that case, the biddy needs to go to confession to stop her runaway tongue."

Father Stillmac looked at his watch. "Oh my goodness, I'm late for a meeting. I'll see you later, and thanks for the dinner."

Sam brought the check to Judge Marbling who stated, "I just sold my daughter to this young man for a dollar and a half, give it to him as restitution for getting the second most beautiful girl in town.

Mrs. Marbling teased, "Why thank you kind sir."

Ann Marie puckered, then laughed, put her arms in a circle extended from her stomach and said, "Just wait until I am out to here with your grandson, then you'll rate me as number one."

Mrs. Marbling intervened, "You are number one." She looked at Barton, who was standing. "Don't you agree?" she asked.

CHAPTER 18

Tom Bradleton's Fate

Barton did not have a chance to answer Mrs. Marbling as to his agreement with her choice of number one because some friends had dropped by the table to chat and express congratulations to them on the forthcoming marriage of their daughter.

Even as they exited the lobby to the parking lot, a couple came by and congratulated Ann Marie. She thanked them; waved to her Mother and gave a lip motion that she would see her at the house.

In the car, Ann Marie flipped the toggle switch to the radio. Vaughn Monroe was singing, "Racing With The Moon." She eased over to her fiancé and said, "I feel like racing with the moon. My whole body is tingling. Is there not something that we can do?"

He took her under his right arm, steering with his left, keeping his eyes on the road and traffic about, squeezed her shoulder and responded, "I am not that knowledgeable about such things, why don't you ask your Mother?"

"I believe that I will." She retracted her statement and told Barton, "We'll figure it out."

They got to the house ahead of her parents, went upstairs to the garage apartment, started unpacking the boxes brought from his house, when they heard a door slam with a bang.

And, almost simultaneously they heard three more very loud bangs that sounded like pistol shots. They glanced out of the window but could barely see as the trees that surrounded the garage apartment shielded their view. They found an opening, spotted a man running around widow Langur's house. Barton pointed him out to Ann Marie and asked, "Is he carrying a gun, or is that a camera?"

The man with the gun or the camera disappeared at the time lights came on in backyards of several of the neighborhood houses.

They scampered down the stairs and into the yard and on to the screened portico of the main house. As they opened the door, they hesitated. Widow Langur ran from the back door of her house, dressed only in a robe and carrying a blanket. She threw the blanket over an object lying on the ground in her backyard, stopped briefly to restore her robe to her upper body, then rushed back inside her back door.

Judge and Mrs. Marbling came out of the house. "What happened?" When I heard the shots, I called the police."

And, almost that instance, the Police Chief and a deputy drove into the driveway.

They came to the back of the house, asked the Judge from where did the shots come. He pointed to the backyard of the house of Widow Langur.

The Chief walked over to her yard, lifted the blanket, motioned for Judge Marbling to come over. "See if anyone's in there," he said to his deputy, motioning toward the Langur house.

Judge Marbling released his arm from his wife and walked into Widow Langur's backyard. He viewed the dead body. Three different spots of blood oozed slowly from it. It was Tom

Bradleton. He had been shot in the back. He was naked.

The Chief asked Judge Marbling if he would call the Coroner and ask him to meet him at McGilvery's Funeral Home.

He walked to the edge of his yard where his family was observing this bizarre affair. "Let's go inside," he said. "It's Tom Bradleton. He's been shot."

Without looking back, all four entered the house. Judge Marbling went directly to the phone, called the coroner and gave him the message of the Chief of Police. Mrs. Marbling remarked in a subdued voice, "Henry, I do believe that I could use a crème de menthe."

"Me, too." Then in a heartily gesture, he asked, "What about the Sandeaus?"

Ann Marie curtsied and answered, "The Sandeaus kindly accept your offer."

Judge Marbling went to his prized piece of furniture, a dry bar, with a marble top, took from it, four liqueur glasses, a bottle of crème de menthe, and began to pour.

Mrs. Marbling turned on the radio just as Jeremy Vordan began reciting John Gillespie Magee's poem, *High Flight*:

Oh, I have slipped the surly bonds of Earth, And danced the skies on laughter-silvered wings; Sunward I've climbed, And joined the tumbling mirth of Sun-split clouds, and done a hundred things you have not dreamed of — Wheeled, and soared, and swung high in the sunlit silence. Hov'ring there, I've chased the shouting wind along. And flung my eager craft through footless halls of air. Up, up the long delirious, burning blue. I've topped the wind-swept heights and easy grace, Where never lark, or even eagle flew; And while with silent lifting mind I've trod the high untrespassed sanctity of Space, Put out my hand and, And touched the face of God.

Mrs. Marbling, with an emotional gesture, remarked, "I've heard Jeremy recite that poem many times; and each new time that he reads it, he seems to grasp a truer meaning of the thrill of flight." She looked at her husband, lifted her liqueur glass and told him that tomorrow that she was going on the plane with the children to Randolph to help Ann Marie with her things.

"You can't get all of her belongings on that plane," he said.

"We are going to ship her trunk by Railway Express, and bring with us on the plane, just those things she needs in the next few days."

Judge Marbling returned the gesture, lifted his liqueur glass, responded, "While you three are reaching out and touching the face of God, I will be attending Clarabelle's funeral, and more than likely attend the inquest of Tom's murder."

Ann Marie took a sip of her crème de menthe, lifted her liqueur glass, and held it at eye level stating through the dull green liqueur, "We have something else that we want to spring on you two."

Judge Marbling, now in a festive mood, answered, "We know that you are not pregnant, we know that you have not flunked out of school, and we know that we do not know what it is that you two want to spring on these two."

Ann Marie laughed, hugged her dad, winked at her mother, and blew a kiss to Barton. "These two want you two to go with us on our honeymoon. We are going to fly to Havana, Cuba, in the Stinson."

Mrs. Marbling stood.

The Judge sat down.

Barton echoed, "We really mean it. We'll get married at the

10 o'clock Mass on Saturday, and plan to depart shortly after noon."

Judge Marbling got up, moved next to his wife, took her chin in his hand, planted a big kiss on her lips.

"Why not."

She widened her eyes, fluffed her hair, and remarked, "Why not. We certainly are not spending much money on the wedding. We could treat our dear children to this trip to Havana."

Judge Marbling looked at Barton and said, "I agree, these two treat."

Barton opened his jacket about halfway and gave the Judge a "we can handle it" look.

The Judge retorted, "I know you two are loaded, but I am going to do you like you did Maudie Jefferson."

Barton grinned, "Not that."

Ann Marie said, "Not what?"

The Judge said, "Forget it."

Mrs. Marbling said, "No, we won't, will we Ann Marie?"

Ann Marie walked over to her fiancé, put her nose up to his and with those wide blue eyes, gave him a stern look, stepped back a little, took his lapels, eased them open, as if she was doing a strip tease act, reached into his inside pocket, brought forth the certified check, took one look, puckered her lips, slid it back into the pocket, turned to her mother and said, "These two accept you'se two's offer, because we'se two wants you'se two to make the trip with us."

Mrs. Marbling quizzically spoke, "Now, everybody, but me, knows about that paper in Barton's jacket."

Ann Marie reached inside the pocket, brought out the certified check, walked over and showed it to her mother.

CHAPTER 19

The Gossip

It had been along day, a day which brought many varied events. Barton was ready for his bath and bed. He stripped his clothes, went into the bathroom, drew the water in the cast iron tub that stood above the floor on four heavy ornate legs; checked the temperature of the water, and turned off the spigots.

The water was tepid when he stuck his leg over the edge of the tub, then the other leg, and slowly lowered himself into the water that covered his entire body except his head. He closed his eyes and let his entire being soak.

He was drowsing when a slight tap came upon the door to the bathroom. Immediately, he awoke and sang out, "Come in." The door eased open and there stood Ann Marie and her parents. She walked in, knelt besides the big cast iron tub, stuck her hand into the soapy water that shielded his body; made a splash upon his face, and said, "We want you to come to the house and sleep in the guest bedroom. We don't want you to be alone."

Barton started to object when she went nose to nose with him and her big blue eyes firmly fixed on his, and in between kisses, she said, "The Judge has spoken, so get dressed and we'll wait for you." She sashayed out of the bathroom knowing full well that he was watching her every move.

He hurriedly completed his bath, pulled the drain plug, as the water level lowered, he took the bath cloth and cleaned the dirty ring that had formed. The tub was spotless. He dried himself, realized that his clothes were in the bedroom, and yelled for Ann Marie, "I need some help."

She opened the door, handing him his pajamas and housecoat. "No need to get dressed twice."

Dressed in his sleeping attire, he left the bathroom, joined the Marblings in the small sitting room, thanked them for inviting him to stay at their house. "I don't mind being alone; however, it will be nice to be in a house with someone else."

Arm in arm, all four — two Marblings, one Sandeau, and one about-to-be Sandeau, walked the short distance to the screened portico. At the portico, Barton realized that all of them were dressed in pajamas and housecoats.

Judge Marbling was the last to enter. He latched the door, went into the kitchen where the table was set for milk and cookies.

"A relaxing repast for a busy day," chimed Mrs. Marbling as she poured the milk.

In between sips of milk, Judge Marbling asked, "Tell us about your school plans."

Ann Marie stood up, curtsied as she opened her blue silk house coat, answered: "My dear father, my dear beloved father, my dear beloved and generous father, who offered to sell his only daughter into bondage, for the meager sum of one dollar and fifty cents, American; to this specimen of the opposite gender; who now inquires of our plans, to which he is entitled, since he has agreed to go with us on our honeymoon, be advised . . ."

Her mother laughed, "You may close your robe now, your breasts are showing."

Judge Marbling glanced at Barton with an amused smile,

noticed that he was neither embarrassed, nor surprised at the remarks of Mrs. Marbling, and then addressed Ann Marie, "My dearest daughter, please reveal your plans and not your beautiful body."

Ann Marie went into her belly dance routine, floated lightly on her toes toward her father, hugged his neck, kissed him on the forehead, and continued her speech.

"My adorable father, please be advised, that this gorgeous bedfellow of yours [she moved to her mother and kissed her on the cheek] and this gorgeous soon-to-be the bedfellow of mine, are going tomorrow, to Lynchburg, to terminate my confinement, at that girls school." She moved to Barton, hugged him, kissed him passionately on his lips. Her lingering kiss was soon interrupted by a cough from her mother who said, "Mr Sandeau, I do believe that you are getting a spoiled brat for a wife."

Ann Marie knew that she had teased enough when her mother had spoken, so she again hugged her mother and asked, "And who spoiled me?" Then she asked, "Were you as eager to marry daddy as I am Barton?"

Before she could answer, Judge Marbling chirped, "She sure was. The only difference is that our parents were so Puritanical that we would not dare kiss in front of them." He looked admiringly at his wife and continued, "But, we do think that it is healthy and wholesome for young people to express themselves in the presence of their parents."

Ann Marie hugged her daddy as she responded.

"I am glad that I was born to you two gorgeous people." She noticed that Barton had flinched when she uttered "two gorgeous people" so she picked up the glasses and plates, carried them to the sink and began washing them.

Mrs. Marbling spoke to Barton in a motherly tone, "The

guest bedroom is opposite ours upstairs. When you are ready, the Judge and I will show you where it is."

Ann Marie turned around and held up her two soapy hands. "At least you guys could help with the dishes."

Judge, Mrs. Marbling, and Barton jumped up and went to the sink.

Ann Marie washed. Barton dried, handed them to the Judge who handed them to Mrs. Marbling who placed them in the cabinet.

When they were finished with the dishes, Ann Marie moved to her mother and whispered, "I'll show him where the guest bedroom is."

Mrs. Marbling gave her that "but-you-are-not-married" look, then remarked, "Oh! What the hell!" She took the Judge's arm and said. "If we are going to get an early start on the 'morrow, let's get some sleep."

The four of them climbed the stairs. The Judge and Mrs. Marbling went to their room. Ann Marie went with Barton to the guest bedroom.

Mrs. Marbling began a slow pace on her carpeted floor, then stopped and gave the Judge a "what-do-we-do" look, then paced some more. Soon the Judge took her by the arm, led her into the spacious rectangular hall where at once they saw a light shining from the partially opened door of the guest room. They eased over and peeked in. What they saw overcame their doubts and suspicions.

They tapped on the door and responded to Ann Marie's beckon to join them.

The Judge knelt beside Barton, Mrs. Marbling knelt beside Ann Marie, and the four of them continued Praying the Rosary.

When they had finished praying the Rosary, Barton made the

sign of the cross, raised himself from the bedside, thanked the Judge and Mrs. Marbling for joining them.

Ann Marie was having a small problem getting the sign of the cross. Barton reached around her, took her hand and executed the sign of the cross. She, without any help, did make the sign of the cross. She was pleased. And, Barton was pleased. Several times while the confab was in session, Ann Marie would touch her forehead and recite, "In the Name of the Father." Then she would touch her lower chest and recite, "The Son," and then she would touch the left side of her chest and recite, "The Holy Spirit." Then she would touch the right side of her chest and recite, "Amen."

Once more she made the sign of the cross, looked at her parents, observed that they too were making the sign of the cross. Barton explained. All who believe in the Holy Trinity — the Father, the Son, and the Holy Spirit (often recited as the Holy Ghost} will have little difficulty in making the sign of the cross.

Mrs. Marbling spoke, "That is beautiful. And, my young son-to-be, if you are going to pilot that plane tomorrow, you need some sleep." She kissed him on the cheek, looked at Ann Marie, and added, "Young lady, you get to bed. You will have plenty of time for our Barton when you are married."

Ann Marie lay restless in her bed thinking about what the future would hold for her, and for the man that she so dearly loved. In no time, she was snoring.

Mrs. Marbling put her arm across Judge Marbling's chest, whispered into his ear, "Henry, how could Ann Marie be so lucky. In fact, how could we be so lucky. He seems so all alone, yet, he makes no apology, nor does he ask any special consideration."

Barton awoke at 5:30, as was a habit of his for quite some

time. The early morning hours allowed him time to plan his day in a leisurely manner. He slipped on his house coat, silently descended the stairs, made his way into the kitchen, stopped long enough to plug in the coffee pot which Mrs. Marbling had prepared the previous evening.

He quietly unlatched the screen door, eased out of the main house, did a look around the yard, made his way to the garage apartment where his approach plates, en route charts, sectional maps, E-6-B Computer, and all the other items, including those taken from his safety deposit box, were resting in a small brief case.

He took out the contents of the small brief case, laid them on the table, then decided that he would brush his teeth, shave, shower and get dressed for the day. This he did, in a total of fifteen minutes.

Dressed and refreshed and eager to get his day moving, he took the sectionals and spread them on the table, drew a straight line direct from Deer Hill to Lynchburg, drew lines 90 degrees to the nearest VOR stations adjacent to his on course line, plotted the indicated airspeed time to Lynchburg, and began plotting tic marks every ten miles along this direct line; and, identifying landmarks in that area.

A slight tap came to the door at the head of the stairs. He turned, reached the knob, opened the door. There stood Judge Marbling with two mugs of hot coffee.

Barton greeted the Judge. "Good Morning, sir," he said, taking the mug which the Judge had thrust toward him.

"Good morning," he uttered, "And what does flying look like today?"

"Oh! I have not called Flight Service yet; I have just started plotting our course. Even though we are going IFR, I want to plot our course on the sectionals so that Ann Marie and Mrs. Marbling can track our progress."

Judge Marbling, very interested in Barton's methodical way of putting a tic mark every ten miles, asked, "Can those landmarks be seen from the air?"

"On a clear day, they can be seen from very high altitudes. We will be at 5000 feet above sea level and they should be identified without much difficulty. They should be seen very distinctly, too." He paused to take a sip of coffee. "I'll actually be navigating on the radio beams of the Omni range; but, I will also be checking those landmarks just in case I lose my radios."

"How long will the flight take?"

"Lynchburg is 480 air miles from Deer Hill. Our indicated airspeed will be 135 miles per hour, so I have computed actual flying time to be three hours and thirty minutes. That could vary according to the wind effect. And, I have planned a 'comfort stop' at Greenville, S.C. That should take not more than thirty minutes; so for estimating purposes our flight up, should be four hours. The return flight should be about the same, of course, depending on the winds."

"That means you will get there around noon-time," surmised the Judge.

"Don't overlook the time change," reminded Barton.

"Okay, one o'clock," responded the Judge as he gave Barton a confident smile of friendship and stated, " I don't want to meddle in your business, but have you chosen a bank, yet?"

"You're not meddling. I thought that I would use the bank that you use."

The Judge picked up the empty mugs. "I'll let you get back to your flying. And, breakfast should be ready in about twenty minutes." Then, he left the garage apartment, made his way to the main house, into the kitchen where he found Mrs. Marbling in tears, and Ann Marie in a very foul mood. He wondered what on this earth has gone wrong in such a short time. He asked, "What seems to be the matter with you two?"

"I'm going to go over there and pull every bit of the old bitch's dyed hair out, then, I am going to put pepper sauce in her wretched mouth, and I may just stuff it with toilet paper." Then she relaxed and grinned, "Recently used toilet paper."

Mrs. Marbling wiped her tears and told the Judge that old Mrs. Bydian had phoned a moment ago raising all kind of hell about our upstanding family stooping so low as to allow our daughter to marry, not only a bastard child, but even worse, a Catholic.

Judge Marbling gathered both of them into his arms and advised, "Calm down. On second thought, sit down and tell me the whole thing."

Mrs. Marbling continued, "She indicated that she had already called the Reverend and demanded that he put us out of the church. She snorted and said 'And, If he don't, I'm going to get the Deacons to dismiss him.' She continued ranting, 'I can't get in touch with my son, Paul; but, as soon as I do, I am going to make him call a meeting of the Board of Directors of the Club, have them declare us unfit, and immediately terminate your membership.'"

Judge Marbling started a very awkward frown, then a gentle smile and asked, "Was that all?"

Ann Marie respectfully answered her father, "No, sir. She bellowed that she was looking for the members of the Legislature to request that they not only remove you as a Judge, but disbar you also. She raved on and on. She's a tyrant."

Judge Marbling stood between the two, seated, hugged them,

took a deep breath, "Let's spare Barton all of this crap. I think that I know how to put a stop to it."

He picked up the phone. "Operator."

"Maybelle, this is Judge Marbling. By chance did you overhear Mrs. Bydian's threats to my wife?"

"Why Judge, you know we don't listen."

"I know, Maybelle, but you owe me a couple, so tell me what you heard."

"I think the old bitch is insane. That Maudie whats-her-name don't help. She has been calling Mrs. Bydian often, feeding her a bunch of lies, and by the time Mrs. Bydian adds her version, the whole mess becomes ridiculous." Maybelle paused and told the Judge that she had to go; her switchboard was beginning to light up.

He hung up the phone and was about to say something, when Barton came onto the screened portico. The Judge put his finger to his lips to indicate that she should spare him.

Ann Marie met him at the kitchen door, kissed him, hugged him tightly as if to protect, forced a reasonable smile. "Good Morning," she said mildly.

Mrs. Marbling calmly said, "Good Morning, Barton, breakfast is ready."

The four sat down for breakfast. The atmosphere was now a little less solemn; but enough to prompt Barton to ask, "And, is it fair to ask why the gloomy looks?"

Ann Marie answered, "I wish you hadn't asked. But, one thing I will not do is withhold anything from you." She told him about old Mrs. Bydian's phone call.

Barton listened intently.

When Ann Marie had finished about "That ole Tyrant," he stood up, gave a reassuring smile to Mrs. Marbling, who had become more at ease and questionably looked at the Judge. He eased Ann Marie's head slightly backward, kissed her forehead and remained standing while he politely and warmly remarked, "One thing that I, throughout my lonely years, have learned is to ignore such talk and get on with my business. And, believe me, I have endured the likes of the 'Mrs. Bydians' many times."

He leaned over Ann Marie's face, which was still tilted slightly backward, again kissed her forehead, smirked friendly like, and asked, "Look at me. Do I look injured?

Everybody relaxed and broke out in laughter. He sat back down, went nose to nose with Ann Marie, gave her that "I want you look," and firmly stated, "As your husband, I seldom, if ever, will command of you something which is wrong; but I will, and I must, request that you put aside Mrs. Bydian and her ugly, runaway tongue, and put your efforts toward your own life." Then he kissed her, got jelly on his lips which, again, brought laughter.

She stood up, marched in her mock belly dance around Barton's chair, put her arms around his neck, pulled his forehead back, kissed him, and submissively stated, "The Master has spoken." She curtsied and sat down in his lap.

Judge Marbling, still laughing, said, "I don't believe that you two can wait until you get married. Why don't I do the ceremony right now?"

Ann Marie got out of Barton's lap, moved to her father, gave him a big hug, kissed him on the cheek, and politely, but emphatically, retorted, "No. No sir. Sir." She kissed him again on the cheek, looked him in the eye and stated, "Mr. Sandeau and I will be married after Mass on the Saturday forthcoming."

Mrs. Marbling spoke, "You two love birds had better cool it as we will be on that plane about four hours and our pilot needs all of his attention on the flying." She patted Ann Marie on the rump and continued, "If we are going to eat, we had better get our picnic basket packed."

Barton eased over to the garage apartment, brushed his teeth, gathered his maps and other items and placed them in the brief case, tidied the bed, and left for the main house.

As he exited the door of the garage, he heard, "We are on our way." It was Ann Marie swinging the picnic basket, and waving, in a more joyful mood than earlier when he had found them in disgust over old Lady Bydian's phone call.

CHAPTER 20

Lynchburg

Barton took the keys Mrs. Marbling handed him, opened the rear door to her 1948 Chevrolet Sedan, helped her get into the back seat, placed the picnic basket next to her, turned to open the front door for Ann Marie; she was already seated.

She allowed him to shut the door, then rolled down the window and yelled, "Let's go, chauffeur."

He backed the car out of the drive to the street, turned toward North Three Notch, and was, as a habit, a good habit, checked the gauges and eased on the gas. He noticed the ever-present Mrs. Langur on her porch, in her morning cloak, curlers protruding, watering her plants, and peering as if she was insulted that Mrs. Marbling had not apprised her as to where she might be going so early this morning.

Ann Marie, without much thought, remarked, "Well, the old girl has lost another lover."

Mrs. Marbling coughed as if to chastise, but changed her mind, mimicked, "Ann Marie. What theyse do in theyse room is theyse business."

Barton let out a cackle, "Those are exactly my sentiments." And quickly added, "This is a lovely street with perhaps a lot of history."

Mrs. Marbling replied, proudly, "Yes, in days gone bye, it

probably hosted people from all over the world, mainly here, to purchase our cotton." Then she proudly smirked, "And, to capture our Southern Belles."

Barton laughed, "I can certainly relate to that. I have been in Deer Hill not yet a full week and I have captured one of those Southern Belles." He hesitated and said, "Or, I have been captured by one of them."

Ann Marie gave him a slight, friendly tap on the thigh.

Mrs. Marbling echoed, "I think that you are the one who has been captured."

Ann Marie yelled, "Mother!"

Barton gave a slight tap to Ann Marie's upper thigh and sweetly hummed, "But, I did slow down so I could be captured."

Ann Marie balled her fist, playfully retorted, "I am going to capture you, with this."

He stopped for a traffic light at North Three Notch, began to hum as he peered at the beautiful blue sky that he hoped would prevail throughout the day. The traffic light changed, Barton eased the automatic shift into drive, drove to Fairview Street, turned left and waved at Mr. Watkins at Estencrest Filling Station.

Very few words had been spoken until he turned onto the airport road. Ann Marie turned toward Barton and inquired, "Mr. Sandeau, do you now before a witness profess your love for me. To hold. To cherish. To honor. To obey . . . oops, erase that. I'm the one who is supposed to obey."

Barton stopped the car in the parking lot, went nose to nose with her and recited, "Until death do we part." He kissed her on the nose.

Mrs. Wards handed the paperwork to Barton for his signature.

He went out to the Stinson, did the pre flight, walked back to the office, used the rest room, returned, asked his passengers if they were ready.

Everything about the plane was in order, so Barton helped his passengers get aboard. He folded the front passenger seat forward, helped Mrs. Marbling step up, and into the rear of the cabin. Once she was seated in the overstuffed, spacious, sofa-type, high-back couch, with comfortable armrests that served as small lockers for sick packs and other items normally needed from time to time; he helped her with her seat belt. He placed the picnic basket on the couch next to her and secured it. Ann Marie waited for Barton to step aside, then she climbed into the right side of the front seats, fastened her seat belt, reached out, grabbed the door, pulled in shut, latched it leaving the window open.

Barton admired the way she was becoming acquainted with airplanes. He handed her his brief case and said, "Okay Navigator, are we ready for departure?"

Ann Marie saluted, answered, "Aye, aye, Sir," took the check list, began reading each item very carefully and watching Barton perform the check. This time she was more confident, so Barton methodically prepared the plane for takeoff.

He announced over the unicom, "Four Eight Three Alpha George, taxing runway 25, takeoff IFR, Lynchburg."

No other traffic appeared to be in the area, so Barton let Ann Marie taxi the short distance to the warm up apron, went through the procedures, and announced. 483AG, rolling 25.

With ten degrees of flap, the Stinson sped down the runway and rotated into the sky.

Barton flew the prescribed departure patterns until he reached his on course heading.

Ann Marie,scanning the sectional chart, and looking out of

the window to see if she could identify the first check point, raised up in her chair, pointed to the Forest Ranger Tower and remarked, "That's it."

She beamed with a sense of accomplishment and pride, then turned to her mother and helped her to locate same.

Barton held the plane steady, continued his climb toward his requested altitude, and upon reaching 2000 feet, contacted Montgomery Radio for his IFR clearance. He received his clearance and also instructions to contact Atlanta Radio, report reaching 5000 feet.

The plane reached the assigned altitude. Barton leveled her, adjusted trim tabs for stability, switched on the auto pilot, and relaxed.

Ann Marie had identified another check point, found it on the line drawn on the sectional, turned around and showed it to her mother. It was the water tank at Union Springs.

Mrs. Marbling became interested in the navigation and kept a constant lookout for the next landmark which Ann Marie described.

"Okay Navigators. Next procedure is to compute our ground speed. We already know our indicated airspeed." He pointed to the Air Speed Indicator on the panel. He told Ann Marie to time how long it took to get from the current check point which we had just cleared to the next one ahead.

Ann Marie began to stare at her watch. Barton handed her a pencil and said, "It is easier, and more accurate, if you write it down, and when we pass the up ahead check point, write that time down. Then figure the amount of time elapsed between check points."

Ann Marie smugly gave him another aye-aye look and wrote down the time.

Mrs. Marbling had already taken a pen out of her purse and had recorded the time, and was looking for the next check point.

"All right, get ready to record the time as we are coming upon our check point . . . Now," he blared.

"Four minutes," relayed Mrs. Marbling. Simultaneously, Ann Marie stated, "Four minutes."

"Very good," responded Barton. "Now, let's compute our ground speed. Ann Marie take the E-6-B Computer and put the four of the time circle opposite ten on the mileage circle and read the number opposite the big arrow."

Ann Marie had skillfully used the slide rule in some of her math courses, and very quickly grasped the use of the E-6-B, a circular computer. "Wow! We're doing 150 miles per hour."

Barton had mentally calculated the speed by using 4 into 60 is 15 times 10 is 150. He did not, however, override his two navigators efforts; instead, he complimented them and advised that they had a fifteen knot tail wind.

Occupied with the flying and the navigating, they were approaching Greenville, S.C. Barton computed his time in flight to be one hour and forty minutes, and they had covered 232 air miles. He reported this information and remarked, "We can make a 'comfort stop' at Greenville, if you think it is necessary."

Both navigators stated, "I'm fine. Let's go on."

Over Mt. Airy, Barton viewed the chronometer. It was 11:15. He turned to Mrs. Marbling and suggested.

"Stewardess, do you think it is time to serve lunch?"

She smiled, followed Ann Marie's response, and reported, "Aye, aye, sir."

She passed a sandwich to each of them, then a glass of water and a napkin.

Ann Marie held the glass of water for Barton, and remarked,

"The time sure has gone by. I believe that I am going to like this flying."

Mrs. Marbling put her sandwich down, grabbed her pen and shouted, "We're over our check point."

Ann Marie stuck both water glasses between her legs, grabbed her pencil and wrote down the time.

The lunch continued. They had sandwiches, fruit, water, then tea, and then brownies. It took about forty-five minutes to complete the lunch as in-between bites the navigators had learned to use the E-6-B, and both had to double check the other before they would relay the ground speed to the pilot; and the pilot was busy as he had now picked up a cross wind and he needed the use of both hands to keep the airplane steady and on course. The lunch was finished, all items left were returned to the basket. Mrs. Marbling asked, "What is that over there?"

Barton looked at the sectional, checked his omni beam, and proudly announced, "Ladies, we are about to land in Lynchburg."

And, just afterward, the Controller came on the air. "483 Alpha George, descend and maintain 3000, altimeter 29.98."

"Twenty-nine point ninety-eight out of five for three," reported Barton. He gave the vertical trim tab a small downward move to start the descent.

Level at 3,000, he received instructions from the Controller to descend and maintain 2,000, report Lynchburg in sight. Again, he gave a downward move to the trim tab, eased back on the throttle, spotted Lynchburg Airport, picked up the mike, called to the Controller. "483 Alpha George, Lynchburg in sight."

"Roger. 483 Alpha George. No other reported traffic. Flight Plan closed. Contact Lynchburg Unicom ll8.2. Altimeter 30.00"

"30.00" 483 Alpha George.

He switched his frequency to the unicom, called, "Lynchburg unicom. 483 Alpha George, three miles south, landing Lynchburg, say your active runway."

"Usually it takes several transmissions to get a unicom station to answer as most small airports do not have a full-time operator standing by. That leaves the unicom to be answered by someone nearby and most likely doing something else; but, this time at Lynchburg, a reply came on the first effort."

"Stinson Four Eight Three Alpha George runway 35 in use. Wind at 340 degrees, gusting to ten knots. No other reported traffic. Will you need services?"

"Lynchburg, Alpha George, will need fuel. And transportation to the college. We're turning left base for 35."

"Roger Alpha George. No other reported traffic."

On his base leg to 35, at 1800 feet, he started a further descent to 1400 feet, turned to a heading of 350 degrees, reduced her power, engaged ten degrees of flap and started the descent to a landing. He added another ten degrees of flap, further reduced power, while maintaining a comfortable angle of descent, and at the prescribed approach speed. He crossed the threshhold, reversed his flaps until the nose of the plane was level, then a little more as she touched down onto the runway. He applied a little brake, let the engine idle, and taxied to the fuel pumps. He shut her down and secured all the instruments.

The fixed base operator at Lynchburg was at the pumps; and, once the propeller stopped spinning, he moved to the airplane, opened the door, helped Ann Marie, then Mrs. Marbling to deplane to terra firma.

They both headed for the rest rooms.

Barton came around, shook the man's hand, thanked him for ordering the taxi, gave him the service order and stated, "We should not be more than an hour or one hour and a half. We are going to Randolph."

He locked the plane, and headed for the rest room.

In the lounge, Mrs. Marbling asked, "Shall we just leave the picnic basket in the plane? There are still a few goodies left."

"Yes, they should be okay, unless there is something that might spoil."

"Just fruit and a few cookies," reminded Mrs. Marbling.

"That shouldn't spoil." He noticed the cab outside. "If everyone is ready, our transportation is here."

They boarded the taxi. Took the fifteen-minute ride to Randolph College.

It seemed longer to Ann Marie, but finally the taxi stopped in front of the Administration Building where they got out. Barton paid the driver who gave him his card.

Mrs. Marbling and Ann Marie went into the administration building, to the Dean's Office, signed the necessary withdrawal slips, rejoined Barton, who was waiting in the freshly painted hallway.

From there, they crossed the quadrangle to Wright Hall. As they entered, the duty clerk yelled, "Ann Marie Marbling! Is this the guy who is taking you away from our beloved institution and especially from me, Susan Delilah Henry."

"Delilah, you are more vivacious than ever. You are now allowed one small kiss on the cheek of Mr. Barton Talmadge Sandeau, my fiancé, after that, you keep that pretty face at arms length. Or better yet, with your gorgeous chest, you best make that two arms length." Ann Marie rushed to her best friend at Randolph, embraced her, stood back, then embraced her again. She whispered, "Isn't he a doll?"

"You bet!"

Delilah hugged Mrs. Marbling. "It is always so good to see you."

She went to Barton, kissed him on the cheek and informed him, "You've got a spoiled one. She has always said that the right man would come along."

Delilah took the withdrawal papers, glanced at them, turned to Ann Marie and stated, "I packed most of your things in the trunk, and left some things for the suitcase."

She handed Ann Marie a receipt and said, "Come on let's go upstairs and get ready. I have already called maintenance and they should be here soon; also, the Railway Express is on its way." She winked at Barton and whispered, "We'll leave this fine specimen here, but I'll hang an off-limits sign on him."

Ann Marie chuckled, "I could leave mama to guard him." Then she kissed him on the nose and said, "Sorry, partner, you are not allowed above this floor, nor out of this room. Rules of the Trustees."

They were not gone more than ten minutes when down the stairs came the maintenance men carrying the trunk, and Ann Marie carrying the suitcase. Barton walked to the bottom of the stairs, took the suitcase, carried it to the porch and placed it apart from the trunk.

The Railway Express truck drove up, a man got out, checked the tags, unraveled the freight bill and asked Ann Marie to sign.

And right behind the Railway Express truck was the cab which had brought them to the college.

Delilah hugged Mrs. Marbling good bye, then Ann Marie, then she stuck out her hand to Barton who took it, leaned over, kissed her on the cheek, and said, "Goodbye, lovely lady."

They entered the cab and were told that the traffic was pretty heavy on the most direct route to the airport, but he would take another less jammed route so to get them there as soon as possible. He turned his cab westward on River Road, came to an almost empty two-lane road, turned south, and took them directly to the airport.

Barton got out and paid the fare, tipping the driver for being so prompt. He lifted the suitcase and walked a short distance, carefully placing it into the rear baggage compartment. He latched it down so that it would not shift, handed Ann Marie his wallet and asked her to go inside and pay the bill while he pre flight the airplane.

Mrs. Marbling looked pleasingly at Barton. "We plan to pay all the expenses on this trip."

"I certainly appreciate the kind thought, but she just about belongs to me; she and I will take care of this trip. You and the Judge are already set for the Cuba trip expense."

Mrs. Marbling squinted her nose in an approving manner and retorted, "I often wondered what kind of man that she would marry." Then held her hand forth so that Barton could assist her in boarding the airplane. She relaxed in the overstuffed couch in the back seat, buckled her seat belt without any help, and was very comfortably situated when Ann Marie returned with a handful of cheese crackers, three colas which she handed to her mother, then she reached to hand Barton his wallet but it fell to the floor and out dropped a condom.

Mrs. Marbling picked up the condom, reached to hand it to Ann Marie, realized what it was, took a good look to make sure, gave a very indifferent "umph" and handed it to her daughter.

Ann Marie did not bat an eyelash. She took it and put it back into the wallet.

Barton had been busy with his cockpit check and had not noticed the event of the condom, but when Mrs. Marbling had said, "Umph," he turned and asked if she were okay.

She said, "Oh! Yes! And, I am ready to navigate home."

He returned his attention to his instrument panel, set the altimeter to 938 feet above sea level- the elevation of Lynchburg field-cranked the engines and did all the preparations for takeoff. He picked up the mike and announced 483 Alpha George taxing for runway 35 for IFR departure Deer Hill, Alabama.

He checked all systems again, moved into position and announced, "483 Alpha George rolling runway 35." He racked the mike, pushed the throttle forward, let the Stinson roll down the runway, and rotate into the beautiful mid day sunny skies. At 3,000 feet, he got his clearance from Roanoke Flight Service.

Roanoke immediately cleared him out of 3,000 for 6,000, his assigned altitude. He reached 6,000, trimmed her up, confirmed his on course heading, engaged the auto pilot and asked his navigators if they were ready to take us home.

A few fluffy clouds began to gather below them; but they were in luck. The wind had changed. The navigators were reporting a ten mile tailwind. Soon, it went to fifteen miles, and within an hour it was twenty mile per hour.

Mount Airy, was cleared twelve minutes ahead of the plotted time. Greenville ahead of schedule, then Athens. Because of their early arrival, Atlanta Center lowered them to 3,000 to avoid any conflicts.

At 4:50, Deer Hill Airport was sighted. Barton canceled his Flight Plan, called, "Deer Hill Unicom. 483 Alpha George."

Mrs. Wards came on the air. "483 Alpha George. Straight in approach runway 25 approved as we have no other reported traffic."

Ann Marie spotted her father's car, looked at Barton, who understood, handed her the mike and showed her the button to depress. She keyed the mike, "Mrs. Wards, is there a handsome man nearby by the name of Marbling?"

"Sure is, Ann Marie, but he has walked out to the ramp."

Barton smoothly maneuvered 483 Alpha George to the runway, taxied to the second intersection where he told Ann Marie to put her feet on the pedals and take us to the fuel pumps.

She did it much to his satisfaction.

CHAPTER 21

The Visitation

Ann Marie taxied the Stinson perfectly, but when she got near the pumps, Barton took over and maneuvered it next to the gas pumps, pulled on the parking brake, told Ann Marie to pinch together the red lever and pull her all the way out.

With preciseness of an experienced pilot, she pulled the fuel mixture control all the way back and listened as the engine came to a stop, and very soon afterward the propeller stopped spinning.

Barton started to open the door when Ann Marie tugged him, pulled him toward her, kissed him passionately, withdrew and whispered, "For the both of us, mama and me."

He secured the cockpit, opened the door on his side, got out, went around to open the passenger side door. It was already open and Ann Marie was on the ground. He smiled, pushed the chair forward, and assisted Mrs. Marbling to deplane.

Judge Marbling, standing near by, waited for his wife to get both feet on the ground, put his arms around her, gave her a big kiss, stated, "That was a fast trip." He kissed her again and asked, "How was the flying?"

She smiled and responded, "It was great. I learned to navigate, and we ate all the food, and we had the best pilot in the world." She turned, hugged Barton, took the picnic basket which he was holding, handed it to the Judge.

She put her arm in his, began walking toward the hangar, stopped briefly, looked at him and said, "You will love our flying trip to Cuba. And, we'll just have us another honeymoon, too."

Judge Marbling looked sincerely at his wife, whispered, "Can't wait that long for a honeymoon with you." Then added, "I missed you, today. In fact, I missed all three of you and wished that I could have been with you on the trip."

Mrs. Marbling swooned into his dark eyes. "We missed you, too. And, I can't wait that long either. And, I know that our daughter couldn't either if she were not in her cycle. I am certain that she knows man." She told him about the condom falling out of Barton's wallet; and, that Ann Marie was not surprised, as she very methodically put it into the wallet before returning it to him.

The Judge laughed with concern, told his wife that it finally dawned on him where he first saw Barton. It was at Lanier's Drugstore, where he purchased a dozen Trojan condoms. He gently squeezed the shoulder of his wife and mentioned, "I believe that we can stop worrying about our dearest; and for certain, her premarital relationships with her fiancé. She is a very lucky young lady to have one like Barton. I love him as a son."

Ann Marie and Barton returned from Mrs.Wards office and rejoined her parents.

"Judge, you shouldn't have paid for this trip."

"Why not. She's still mine."

Ann Marie chimed, "You two stop arguing. I am my own self." Then added, "Barton will pay one way. My dearest father, you may pay the other." Then she hugged them.

Mrs. Marbling echoed, "That is settled. Let's get home." She hugged them.

She turned to Ann Marie. "Why don't we stop by Bob's Bar-B-Q, and get some sandwiches for tonight?"

Judge Marbling added, "And some beer. What kind do you like Barton?"

Ann Marie answered, "We'll take Pabst."

Judge Marbling patted her on the rump. "Do you have an I.D. showing you to be twenty-one?"

Ann Marie chirped, "I've got I.D.s running out of my ears." She patted her father on his rump and spoke, "Just get the beer and sandwiches. We'll meet you at the house."

Judge Marbling opened the car door for his wife, went around got into the driver's seat, waited for Barton and Ann Marie to drive out of the parking lot, followed them onto the highway until he came to Bob's Bar-B-Q. He turned into their parking lot.

The outside waiter came over, took their order for six barbecue and a six pack of Pabst Blue Ribbon.

As they waited for their order, Judge Marbling told his wife about the several visits which he had today. One was Paul Bydian, "Paul wanted to apologize to you, Ann Marie and Barton, but I told him that it was not necessary. He told me that his mother's case had become so deteriorated that he met with Jarvis and they have agreed to have her committed to Brice's. And, they have requested the Probate Judge to hold a sanity hearing in the next few days."

Mrs. Marbling sat in a somber quietness as she listened, but never said a word.

Judge Marbling looked at her and asked, "Hey, pretty lady, why so somber?"

She managed a meager smile, shook her head ambiguously, raised her eyebrows, meekly stated, "That will be a fitting paradox for one who is hell bent on ruining the lives of other people." Then she refrained, "I should not say a thing like that. I truly feel sorry for her." She shook her head again, and asked, "Who were the other visitors?"

Father Stillmac came by to leave a message for Ann Marie. He said that he could not get anyone on the phone at the house. He was downtown, anyway, so he thought I might tell her that 9 o'clock in the morning would be fine."

Before he could tell her about Maybelle's visit, the waiter brought the sandwiches and beer. He paid the waiter, cranked the car, drove homeward with his thoughts of the conversation that he had with Maybelle Floyd, his confidant and able telephone operator.

They arrived home, garaged the car, took the beer and sandwiches into the house where Ann Marie met them, told them that Barton was at the garage apartment putting his papers in order, and that he would be over shortly.

"Yes, he and I have an appointment with the banker tomorrow morning at 8:30; and, I want to invite him to play golf with us in the afternoon, that is, if his spoiled fiancee' will consent."

Mrs. Marbling laughed, "Don't you worry about your sweet spoiled wife fussing about your golf."

"Not, if she agrees that I will not fuss about her bridge." The Judge winked as he spoke.

Ann Marie returned to the kitchen just as the Judge winked at his wife.

She remarked, "You two seem to have the best time together." Then she added, "I'll go fetch my sweet thing."

She walked out of the screened portico, on to the back lawn just as Barton came through the garage door. She ran to him, jumped into his arms, gave him a big hug, kissed him and lovingly said, "Thanks for taking me to Lynchburg. I can hardly wait to be waking up beside you."

Arm in arm they entered the kitchen where Mrs. Marbling was keeping the barbecue sandwiches warm in the oven, and the Judge was opening four of the Pabst Blue Ribbon beer.

For a few moments, no one said a word. They were busy with their delicious sandwiches and cold beer. Finally, Judge Marbling told Ann Marie about the visit from Father Stillmac.

Ann Marie squirmed a little, noticed the askance look on Barton's face, shifted to the edge of her chair, and spoke, "Thanks, Dad. That time will be fine with me." She again looked at Barton and continued, "You know all good Catholics need instructions from the Padre before marrying one of his flock."

CHAPTER 22

Instructions

Ann Marie arrived at the rectory a few minutes before the appointed time of 9 A.M., was about to knock on the door when it opened. A young lady stuck out her hand, took Ann Marie's cordially shook it, and introduced herself as Julia, and proudly stated that she would be studying with her for the Sacrament of Confirmation.

Ann Marie gave her name and asked Julia, "Maybe you can help me as I want to be ready by Saturday morning."

Father Stillmac, in the background, interrupted, saying, "Both of you will have no problem being ready, so let's get started."

"You both have been Baptized, and now the time is here for you to be initiated in the life of adult Christian witness. You will receive the Sacrament of Confirmation which will sustain you in a lifetime of witness to Christ."

He paused a moment as he flipped a few pages, then continued, "You both will kneel at the altar. In unison with the entire congregation, you will repeat the Apostle's Creed. I will ask you to stand. I will moisten my thumb with a specially blessed mixture of olive oil and balsam, and trace the sign of the cross onto you forehead." He explained, "This is the act of laying-on-of-hands which is a procedure dating back to the time of the Apostles. While anointing you, I will call you by your Confirmation name. And say. 'Be sealed with the Gift of the Holy Spirit.'"

He wrote down the confirmation name, chosen by each.

In Ann Marie's case, she chose Ann for St. Ann.

Julia chose Catherine for Saint Catherine.

Father Stillmac, again, addressed the two candidates for confirmation, remarked, "After the Confirmation, we will celebrate the Eucharist. After which I will welcome Ann Marie into the Church, then Julia into the adult life of the Church." He checked his notes, looked at Ann Marie and asked, "Will you want to remove the chrism from your forehead before we perform he marriage?"

"No. Father. I want Barton to join me at the altar as soon as possible, and I want the marriage vows repeated before all who are present."

"So be it." He remarked then asked each of them the name of their sponsor.

Ann Marie told Father Stillmac that she had asked Mr. and Mrs. Harrison to be her sponsors, and, she did not want Barton to know that she was joining the Catholic Church. She wanted to do it for herself, and did not want Barton to think that she was doing it because that he was Catholic.

Father Stillmac understood and assured her that Barton would only know when he attended Mass on Saturday. He told both candidates that they were ready except for a brief rehearsal; and if Ann Marie desired, they could also rehearse the wedding.

"The wedding rehearsal won't be necessary. I just want to be at his side, say the vows, exchange rings and listen with all my heart when you pronounce us man and wife."

Father Stillmac grinned, "I hope that I don't forget." Then he hugged both candidates around the shoulder and bid them good afternoon.

Ann Marie returned the adieu's to Julia and to Father Stillmac, and headed home to have lunch with her mother. At home, her mother told her that they had been invited to lunch with Mrs. Blackenridge at the Deer Hill Inn at noon.

"That's fine with me." Happily replied Ann Marie, "I'm going to freshen up and change into a more dressy dress." She winked at her mother and continued, "I need to look my best if I am to be in the company of the two most beautiful women in town."

It was fifteen until 12, when the two Marblings left the front door of their house, waved to the ever present, gazing, nosy neighbor-the widow Langur-climbed into Ann Marie's Mercedes, drove to the Deer Hill Inn, parked at the end of the block, locked the car and slowly strolled, arm-in-arm, toward the Inn. Ann Marie told her about the instructions to become a Catholic.

Mrs. Marbling slid her arm around Ann Marie's shoulder, stopped briefly faced her. "I think that is wonderful. Does Barton know?"

"No, ma'am. Not yet. In fact, I don't want him to know too soon. I am doing this for myself." She was about to tell her when it would be that Barton would know, when Sylvester, standing on the sidewalk, held the door open for them. They entered.

There was Mrs. Blackenridge, radiant as ever, looking beautiful attired in a gorgeous blue suit with white trim.

"She deserves her pedestal," Ann Marie mused silently.

Mrs. Blackenridge, ever the gracious and observant lady, embraced Ann Marie, complimenting her attire. "I have not yet met your fiancé so I thought that at lunch, you and Mary Margaret could tell me about him."

Mrs. Marbling replied, "Miriam, you'll love him. He is a good Catholic." She hesitated, gave Ann Marie a motherly apologetic look for answering, then continued, "And I just learned that your church will be getting another good Catholic."

"Ann Marie, I think that is wonderful, but do remember to let your religion be between you and God."

"Exactly my feelings, Mrs. Miriam. I don't want Barton to know until we have the Confirmation on Saturday."

Sam, with his ever-alert eye for guests of the dining room, bowed to the three ladies. "Ladies, please follow me." He led them to a small circular table in the very center of the dining room, as if to make them the main attraction of the day.

Sam took the order, motioned for Moses to bring a carafe of Chablis, went to the sideboard, fetched a beautiful vase of Roses — amber-colored with a scent of a mild pickled peach, named "Whiskey Mac." He placed it on the center table.

The three beautiful ladies, at the center table, were impressed. Sam was wise.

Mrs. Marbling, in old-fashioned ways, described her son-in-law-to-be, as a young man who seems to have his feet on the ground.

Ann Marie chuckled gleefully, "And, he is a young man who has swept my feet off the ground."

The three were laughing, and had just taken their first sip of wine, when in came Sara Lou Bydian and her grandmother who, the moment she spotted the center stage table began to twitch, rant, rave, and snort. She went into a spasm and fell flat on her face.

Sara Lou began wringing her hands, looking desperately for help.

Ann Marie, observed the whole scene with disgust, asked

Sylvester to call the ambulance. Frothing at the mouth, stuttering Sara Lou, skin pale and clammy, perspiring profusely, was in
shock.

After a few soothing words from Ann Marie, and the use of a
moist cloth on her brow, and wrist, Sara Lou sat up in a chair.

The attendants from the ambulance brought into the lobby,
a stretcher on which they placed, ole Mrs. Bydian who was
bleeding from the nose. They gathered her broken speckles,
purse, and straw hat — complete with pink ribbon which
matched the heavy rouge on her cheeks — and gave them to Sara
Lou who had now regained some degree of balance.

In a very pitiful look of total embarrassment, she stood,
leaned against Ann Marie, breathed deeply several times. She
finally mustered her senses with enough energy to say, "Can you
ever forgive us for her behavior?" She managed a wry smile,
paused, erected her posture, perked her lips and sincerely stated,
"When the sanity hearing was mentioned, I went into a dither,
raked my dad over the coals, chastised him for wanting to send
her to a mental institution; but, now I believe that I understand
why it is necessary." She paused again, fluffed her hair, and
added, "We cannot go on trying to cater to her when we know
full well that she is going to show her ass everywhere that she
goes."

Ann Marie put her arm around Sara Lou's shoulder. "Don't
be embarrassed where we are concerned. That comes under the
heading of the business of the family, Bydian."

Sara Lou, now much more reconciled, looked up, "I have
lived under the influence of that tyrant all of my life. She has
held herself out to be the pillar of the community, the church,
our family, and whatever else, but she is nothing but a phony
with a guilty conscience about Jarvis and his multitude of antics

that she has sluiced off as the faults of everybody, but the heralded Mr. Jarvis Bydian." She paused, took another deep breath as if relieved, nodded somberly, wiped her brow and once more and sincerely stated, "After all these years I have finally said that which has been on my mind for a long, long time, but would not because she is my own dear grandmother, and I do love her very much, yet now, in my most stable mental frame of mind, I must agree with father and hereby say: 'let the Sanity Hearings begin.'"

Earlier in the day, Barton, with an able ally Judge Marbling, walked into the offices of Mr. Jackson Y. Chauffi, whose banking reputation, heralded by many, especially himself and his wife, who, like clockwork, spend a portion of each day, visiting with friends, on the telephone party line, somehow, during the course of the usually, one-sided conversation, manage to protect that heraldry. That is, after it was confirmed that she married a man of notable social position, one with an achieving portfolio in banking.

Judge Marbling knew better. He also knew that he could rely upon the esteemed Mr. Chauffi to be true to form, and discreetly leak into the gossip mill, certain, normally confidential, information.

"Jackson, I want you to meet Barton Sandeau who wishes to open an account with your bank."

"It's a pleasure. You know we have a minimum. If it's a check drawn on a foreign bank, you must wait until it clears," he recited like a third grader.

"We have some well-trained tellers who will help you," remarked Mr. Chauffi smugly. He was becoming offended that he, the President of the bank (by virtue of his wife's family holdings) had been reduced, by the Judge, to a chore usually performed by underlings.

"Jackson, if you will steer us to one of those well-trained tellers, Mr. Sandeau will make a substantial deposit." He hesitated then announced, "A certified check."

Mr. Chauffi breached the specs on his nose that had slipped below his eyes, glared at the Judge, then at Barton. "How substantial?"

Barton, on cue from Judge Marbling, handed the certified check to Mr. Chauffi.

"Is your bank insured?"

"What rate of interest does your bank pay?"

In a business-like manner, he inquired as he looked directly into the stolid expression of two twitching eyes, a twitching nose, and almost-rouged flushed cheeks, ears that had become upright, all belonging to the President of the bank, who stared at the check. He paused, glanced at the almost idle teller cages and remarked, "They seem busy. I'll take care of this for you."

Mr. Chauffi, no longer in a hurry, no longer too busy to wait on a customer, no longer offended, and no longer demonstrating his importance, beckoned for his Secretary and gave her the check, directing her to call the bank of issue and obtain an oral confirmation.

Barton reached, again, into his jacket pocket and brought forth a second check.

Mr. Chauffi recovered from his decency posture, resumed his role of importance, began to give instructions to his new bank customer, as to how he might invest his money, and how, he, Mr. Sandeau, could rely on the expertise of "My" bank to guide him through treacherous waters of handling that much money.

The Secretary returned, handed him the two checks, and a

note: "Not only are these two valid; he has considerable more."

Mr. Jackson Y Chauffi, turned pale, breathed heavily for a few seconds, sat down to his desk, and submissively proceeded to open the accounts. An Interest Bearing Pass Book Savings account in the amount of $250,000. at a rate of three and one half percent compounded annually. A second account — a checking account — in the amount of $22,500.

Barton signed the necessary documents. "Mr.Chauffi, sir, Ann Marie will be in to sign the signature of the checking account."

With a big smile, Mr. Chauffi suggested, "Just tell that pretty lady to come by my office. I will assist her in anyway that I can."

As they departed the offices of Mr. Chauffi, whose arm was around the shoulders of one, Barton T. Sandeau, newly acquired customer, obtained by Mr. Chauffi, himself, and whose prodding inquiries, to elicit the whereabouts of the origin of such deposits, fell on deaf ears.

The origin of the money was not revealed.

CHAPTER 23

Latest News

Without another word spoken, Barton, with his checkbook in hand, and Judge Marbling with an achieving smile, left the Italian marble structure of the Merchants Bank.

Outside, Judge Marbling peered across the street to the court house resting in the center of the square, guarded somewhat by the statute of the Confederate Soldier—facing North, returned to his about-to-be son, and remarked, "A number of places were spared by design in that terrible civil war, and I'm glad that Deer Hill was one of them."

He again looked at Barton who had a tear in his eye, then he thought, "Why did I have to make that comment, particularly to one who lost both parents during a war." He put his arm around Barton and said, "I'm sorry. I did not mean to bring up such things that would remind you of your most endeared losses."

"Please, don't apologize. I often, without any prompting, think about them, and the things that we did together." He smiled humbly and continued, "You and Mrs. Marbling have filled a void in my life. You have given me another comfort zone. And," he said turning to Mr. Marbling, "you are giving me your most prized possession."

A tear came to Judge Marbling's eyes as he smiled with a great deal of pride. "We're not losing a very fine and precious daughter, we are gaining a son which we have so long wished for; but, could never have until Ann Marie brought you to us, and . . ."

He did not get to finish because the Circuit Clerk came and told him that the Sheriff needed him at the court house.

Judge Marbling reminded Barton of the lunch date, and the golf game at one, then left for the Sheriff's Office in the Court House across the street in the Square.

Barton stood for a moment gazing at the statute of the Confederate Soldier, then decided that he would go across the street and purchase a suit for his wedding.

As he entered the department store, his friend, Mr. Albert, met him at the door and shook his hand. "Playing with us today?"

Barton replied, "Looking forward to it. I need a suit for my wedding."

Mr. Albert led him to the men's department, began to search for a particular suit, finally pulled from the rack, a dark blue serge, almost a black, double-breasted suit, size thirty-eight. He held the coat open for Barton to put on, then asked, "How do you like this?"

Barton tried on the pants and Mr. Albert pinned the cuffs, then went to the shirt rack, brought a Gellersmeldt shirt, size-sixteen collar and thirty-two-inch sleeves. Before he handed it to Barton, he asked, "What size do you wear?"

"Sixteen collar, thirty two sleeve."

They were searching the tie rack when Mr. Albert's brother came in, walked up, introduced himself, glanced at the suit on the counter, and without hesitation picked out a gold-and-black-stripped tie, handed it to Mr. Albert. Barton laughed, "That's It." Mr. Albert carried the shirt and tie to the counter, made a slip out to Barton T. Sandeau, sent the suit to the tailor for alteration and pressing. He attached a note that he needed it ready for delivery on Thursday.

Barton looked around the department store a little more, then went to the counter and asked Mr. Albert how much he owed. Mr. Albert asked if he wanted to open an account and then told him that he could use their easy payment plan.

Before he could answer, Mr. Albert's brother whispered into his ear.

Mr. Albert gave a big broad smile and said, "My apologizes sir, my brother has just returned from the Westside Cafe and the news is out that you have deposited a considerable sum of money in the bank."

"News does travel fast, don't it." Then he quipped, "I'll use my easy pay plan." He wrote them a check.

Mr. Albert walked with him to the door. They were about to go out on to the sidewalk when the Police Chief came up and asked Barton to come with him and told him that the tires on his car had been slashed.

Mr. Albert overheard the Chief's remarks and asked, "What low-life has done such a thing?"

The Chief said, "We think that it is that Palomino and his weird sidekick Plaster."

Barton went with the chief to the parking lot in the square and there was his prized 1933 Plymouth with all four tires flat as a fritter.

Judge Marbling, the Sheriff, the Circuit Clerk and others were standing about.

Judge Marbling asked, "Barton, do you want to swear out a warrant?"

Barton, in a very subdued tone, answered, "No sir. As long as they are only suspects, let's leave them alone." He solemnly added, "I'll walk over to Goodyear and get them to put me four new ones on."

He walked a few steps, turned, addressed the Judge, "Sir, I expect that I will have to take a rain check on the lunch and the golf."

Barton wrote a check for the new tires. He had the slashed tires put in the back. He glanced at his watch. It was now 12:30. He decided that he would go to Deer Hill Inn and have some lunch.

He parked on the side next to a black Pontiac that had a sign on the back window with a word "Palomino." He thought it was just a coincidence, but changed his mind when he was met by Sylvester who told him that Miss Roxy had called for Mrs. Marbling. It seems someone had broken into the garage apartment, smashed the dishes and the crystal, and disrupted all of the furniture. They also stole the silver.

Sylvester continued, "The ladies left without finishing their lunch." Then, in a slightly nervous tone, he reported, "And, that Palomino fellow is sitting in the lobby with a smirk on his face as if he has done conquered the world. He knows that it is Wednesday and the Inn is usually quiet, and he can have his time with that nymph, Mrs. Maudie." He shook his head and peered at Barton. "He has already been up there twice, and now that Plaster is with her. No wonder Mr. Jefferson caught the train a while ago."

Still shaking his head, he followed Barton into the lobby and watched as Barton went directly to within two feet of the chubby, toothless, man with unruly, long bleached hair, rumpled greasy trousers with two of the buttons missing, and addressed him.

"Mr. Palomino, I understand that you have a fancy for slashing tires."

Palomino looked from behind his magazine, jumped up, reached into his pocket as if to find a knife.

It was too late. Barton sent a swift kick to his groin. When Palomino bent down to grab his crotch with his left hand, Barton sent a swift knee to his chin. Palomino reeled backward with his right hand still in his pants pocket. His head snapped back with his beady eyes glaring as if he was in shock. Barton quickly moved in and gave him a tremendous knuckle slice to his protruding Adam's apple. Palomino fell hard to the floor. He was unconscious. Barton's martial arts classes had served him well.

Barton reached down, tied Palomino's shoe strings together, took off his belt with silver buckle, tied his arms behind him, and drug him by his long hair to the parking lot beside his car. He took three of the slashed tires and placed them over his head.

With his right hand still in his pocket, the three slashed tires binding him to his waist; it would be difficult for the still-unconscious Palomino to move.

Sylvester had followed all the moves with a glee and a great deal of pride in the quiet manner in which Barton had done a job on the spiteful Palomino. He grinned at Barton and took from his pocket a key to room 216.

Sylvester eased the key into the lock and quietly moved the door open.

Plaster, with one leg in his pants, looked shocked. He slumped to the floor as Barton had crossed his chin with a forearm and elbow.

And just as swift, Barton took the pants leg and bound one arm of Plaster, and with the belt (also with a silver buckle) he tied the other arm around his neck. Plaster could not move without stretching his neck backwards.

All the while, in the few seconds it took Barton to put a lock and key job on Plaster, Mrs. Maudie, nude—her exposed breasts dangling—with her hands tied to the bed posts, also in shock at what had just taken place, began cursing. When she spotted Sylvester, she yelled, "I'm going to have Palomino beat you to within an inch of your life."

Plaster awoke, blurted, "And when I get loose, I'm gonna . . ."

That was as far as Plaster got with his threat. Barton sent the heel of his shoe to his mouth. Four teeth fell to the floor.

Seeing what happened to Plaster had a sobering effect on the lady lying naked tied to the bed posts. She began to cry and beg for her clothes.

Barton had not smiled since he first saw the slashed tires on his car in the square, but now he smiled at his old friend, picked up Mrs. Maudie's clothes, walked over to the window, and tossed the clothes to the street.

He turned, picked up a sheet, and threw it over Mrs. Maudie Jefferson, politely remarking, "You look better with this on you."

Plaster awoke, began spitting blood, yelled, "I'll kill both of you . . ." And, that was when four more teeth fell to the floor, and he went back to sleep. Barton took Plaster's shirt, tied a sleeve to each of his bare feet, began to drag him out of the room, down the hall, and when he got to the marble stairs, he kicked him in the groin and sent him rolling down the stairs, into the lobby, and into the waiting grasp of the Chief of Police.

Judge Marbling came into the lobby with the Sheriff who immediately asked the whereabouts of Mrs. Jefferson.

Sylvester handed them to the key to room 216. In no time, the Judge, the Sheriff, and Mrs. Jefferson were coming down the stairs. Mrs. Jefferson was clad only in a sheet, carrying her purse.

Barton had walked out on the street, gathered the clothes which he had thrown out of the window, came back into the lobby and handed them to Mrs. Maudie Jefferson.

The Sheriff allowed Mrs. Jefferson to go into the ladies restroom to put on her clothes. After about thirty minutes, she had not come out. The Sheriff summoned a maid to go in and check to see if something was wrong. The maid came out screaming.

Mrs. Maudie Jefferson was dead.

CHAPTER 24

Two Confessions

Sheriff Rivers walked over to Barton and put his arm around his shoulder and remarked, "I could use a deputy like you." He removed his arm from Barton's shoulder, reached down, took hold of the shirt tied to Plasters legs and began dragging him toward the door.

Plaster was bawling deliriously and whimpering that he had done nothing wrong to bring all this on. Sheriff Rivers just kept on moving toward the outside door. He put Plaster next to Palomino, who was coming out of his induced slumber.

Palomino was coughing, spitting blood, almost choking. He was frightened.

He saw Sheriff Rivers pushing Plaster's limp body up against the car. He quieted some as he remembered the last session that he, himself, had with the Sheriff.

Sheriff Rivers opened the door to Palomino's car. Under the front seat was the mahogany chest with the silver in it. As he drug the chest from under the seat, a pistol came out with it. It was a .38 caliber, the same caliber that was used to murder Tom Bradleton.

He took one tire off Palomino and put it over Plaster's head, took a second tire off and sat on it. Straddling the slashed tire, Sheriff Rivers reached into his holster and pulled out his slap jack which was about sixteen inches long and made of black leather encasing a piece of steel one half inch wide, one quarter inch thick, and fifteen inches long.

According to Sheriff Rivers it is the best instrument known to elicit the truth from a person; particularly a hoodlum.

"Palomino, take your hand out of your pocket and bring that knife out with it," sternly spoke Sheriff Rivers.

Palomino raised the one remaining tire off of his right arm, brought his hand out of his pocket, and with it a switch blade knife about ten inches long.

"Open the knife, Palomino, place it in that slash on the tire around your neck." He paused a moment, looked disgustingly at the two shaggy truants, rubbed his chin, gazed at the slashed tires and continued, "Let's see just how you boys slash tires. Put it in the rear tire of your car."

"Ah, Sheriff. Them tires are new. What you want me to ruin 'em for?" murmured Palomino.

"Well, I just thought that you and Plaster like to slash tires so much that you could keep in practice on your own car tires."

Palomino hesitated too long. The slap jack came across his nose. It spurted blood all over his already soiled clothes.

"Do it. You don't mind destroying other peoples property, so do it." Sheriff Rivers said as he raised the slap jack and hit Palomino across the buttock; and, kept hitting him each time that he paused while crawling around his car. When all four tires were appropriately slashed, Sheriff Rivers asked, "How much money did you boys get for slashing the tires on the Plymouth?"

"Nothing," said Palomino."

"I am going to ask you one more time." Spoke Sheriff Rivers in a firm, quiet sort of tone, "How much." as he raised the slap jack.

Palomino fainted.

Sheriff Rivers patted the slap jack on his thigh, moved it to a position under Plaster's chin, forced his head slightly upward, stated, "Plaster, I don't believe that you have ever felt this slap jack. It helps people to remember. Now, tell me how much?"

Plaster cried, hissed through the opening where eight teeth used to be, "Don't hit me. I'll tell you all about it. The whole thing."

Sheriff Rivers summoned Sylvester who was standing just inside the door and observing, with silent glee, the proceedings, "Yes. Sir. Sheriff?" he answered.

"Please bring me a pail of water."

He turned to the Chief of Police and asked him if he would go to the courthouse and get the Court Recorder to come with his equipment. Then remarked to the Judge."We are about to listen to a couple of hoods with a bizarre story; and a confession."

Judge Marbling remarked, "I know that if I am here listening to this story, that I will have to recuse myself from any hearing or any trial. I believe that I'll listen."

Sylvester brought the water, gave it to Sheriff Rivers who turned and poured it on Palomino's head.

Palomino came to with his eyes rolling. He saw Sheriff Rivers, and fainted again.

Another bucket of water brought Palomino around. He sat up, leaned against the slashed rear tire on his car, hung his head between his knees, crying.

"Boys, I believe you know the Chief of Police. This gentleman is Judge Marbling.

"And, this gentleman is a Court Recorder. He is going to take your statements. And believe me, we are all going to be right here until we hear the whole story about you, the slashed tires, the break in at Judge Marbling's garage apartment, your involvement with Mrs. Maudie Jefferson, and all else."

The Sheriff looked at Plaster and continued, "So, now tell us your story from the beginning."

Plaster looked at Palomino, then the slap jack, and slowly started his story.

"Back yonder, me and Palomino met this Miss Maudie at the Top Hat Club. She flirted with us and soon we left in her car and went to a cabin on the river. We spent the night with her and she gave us ten dollars. It seems that she had spells where she would look for us and we would do the same thing. She called and told us to meet her at the lodge. When we got there, we saw Mr. Tom Bradleton leaving, and we were about to go up there when we saw Mrs. Clarabelle Bradleton driving up the road. We watched. We saw Miss Maudie leave in a big hurry. Mr. Tom Bradleton come back, and the next thing we saw was Mr. Tom carrying Miss Clarabelle to the car. She seemed like she was hurt."

Sheriff Rivers looked a little startled and turned to Judge Marbling and asked, "Do you recall the time of death that the autopsy showed?"

"I think it was around 10:30." He raised his eyebrows and stated. "Tom had Clarabelle at the hospital around 12:30." Again, raised eyebrows, "So, what happened during that two hours difference." queried Judge Marbling.

"We'll just have to find out," replied the Sheriff.

He faced Plaster. "All right, Plaster, continue with your story."

"This Miss Maudie is a nymph. She told us that she had been with Mr. Tom Bradleton many times while her sister was dating him. And, that she never stopped seeing him, even after Miss Clarabelle married him. We believe that they were together at the lodge, and that Miss Clarabelle was trying to catch them so that she could force Mr. Tom to give her money for her booze habit."

Plaster hesitated a moment, wiped his mouth with the sleeve of his already dirty, bloody, shirt; looked at Sheriff Rivers and asked, "Could I have a drink of water?"

"When you have finished your story."

Plaster continued, "We saw Mr. Tom leave. Miss Clarabelle come up and went inside, then Miss Maudie come out in a hurry."

Chief Halsum asked, "And you think that Miss Maudie hit Mrs. Clarabelle on the head?"

"Yeah, I do," smarted Plaster.

The slap jack went across his already battered mouth. Sheriff Rivers reminded him, "You mean Yes. Sir! Don't you?"

Plaster could hardly talk but he did manage a very low murmur of yes sir.

Sheriff Rivers looked at Palomino, told him to finish the story.

Palomino was shaking, stuttering, sniffling, but, after glancing at the slap jack, began to talk. "What Miss Maudie learned was that she was not the only one seeing Mr. Tom. That widow, Miss Langur, would go over to visit Miss Clarabelle, pretend to be drinking with her, wait for her to pass out from the booze, ease out of the house, back to her house and be with Mr. Tom.

"Miss Maudie was mad. She was furious when we saw her. She took that gun there from her purse, then put it back, went to her car, got a camera, got us to ease over to widow Langur and get some pictures of Mr. Tom and Miss Langur while they were in bed. I snapped three pictures. Mr. Tom got up and grabbed his clothes and ran out the back door. That's when I heard the shots outside. That's when Mr. Tom got shot."

"Who shot him?" asked Sheriff Rivers.

Palomino, still quivering, answered, "I don't know if it was Miss Maudie or Miss Langur."

"What did you do next?" asked Chief Halsum.

"I slipped out the side door, walked about two blocks to where Plaster was waiting in the car. We drove off to the Top Hat Club."

"How did the .38 pistol get into your car?" Asked Chief Halsum.

"I'm not sure. But Miss Maudie came to the Top Hat Club, got us to go with her in her car. We went down by the river and spread a blanket."

Sheriff Rivers pondered a few seconds then asked the Chief and the Judge if they wanted to ask any more questions. Both said no.

Sheriff Rivers motioned for the Deputy to bring the car around. He put Palomino and Plaster in the back seat, and told the Deputy to ride back to the office with Chief Halsum.

Chief Halsum smiled at the Judge and remarked, "Look at Rivers. He put both of them in the back seat, not even cuffed, just hoping that they will make a move to escape, so that he can save the State a lot of money for a trial."

Judge Marbling pretended not to hear. He shook hands with the Chief, and left.

He wanted to find Barton.

Barton had left the Inn immediately after he had returned Miss Maudie's clothes.

He went directly to the church to find Father Stillmac.

In the Confessional, Barton made the sign of the cross and responded "Amen" to Father Stillmac's invitation to have faith in God. He told of his sin in battering the two at the Inn; the provoking reason, and a few other details.

Father Stillmac paused a moment, then assigned a worthy penance of prayer. Barton responded with a prayer of sorrow.

"O My God, I am heartily sorry for having offended you. And, I detest all of my sins, because of your just punishments; but, most of all because they offend you, my God, who are all good and deserving of all of my love. I firmly resolve, with the help of your grace, to sin no more and to avoid the near occasion of sin."

Father Stillmac placed his hands on Barton's head and prayed.

"God, the Father of Mercies, through death and Resurrection of his Son has reconciled the world to himself and sent the Holy Spirit among us for the forgiveness of sins; through the Ministry of the Church may God give you pardon and peace and I absolve you from your sins. In the name of the Father. And, the Son. And of the Holy Spirit. Amen."

Father Stillmac sat silent in the confessional for a few seconds then chimed.

"The Lord has freed you from your sins. Go in peace."

CHAPTER 25

Sanity Hearing

Barton drove into the driveway behind Judge Marbling who was sitting in his car listening to a radio broadcast. He walked toward the Judge's car.

Judge Marbling got out, left the door open so that he could hear the news flash, and at the same time check on Barton. "How you doing?" "Hold on, this is something startling." They both listened.

"We interrupt the program in progress to bring you this news. Ten minutes ago, at the county jail stockade, on Love Street, two prisoners jumped Sheriff Rivers, who had opened the rear door for them to get out of his patrol car. One of them had a gun. According to sources at the scene, the prisoner raised the gun to fire on Sheriff Rivers. Sheriff Rivers fell to the ground, pulled his revolver from its holster and fired twice. One bullet killed the prisoner with the pistol. The second bullet lodged in the upper abdomen of the other prisoner who was taken to General Hospital where he died. On his death bed, he told the detective that they found the pistol in the back of the patrol car, and when his partner fired it, it only clicked. It was empty.

He also told the detective that it was fully their intent to kill Sheriff Rivers."

Judge Marbling turned off the radio. Shaking his head, he

mumbled, "I guess Rivers got his wish."

He closed the car door and turned to Barton. "How are you doing?'

"I'm fine, sir. I left the Inn and went to see Father Stillmac. Everything's fine now."

"How about yourself?"

The Judge put his arm around Barton, humbly stated, "Maybe I would feel better if I went to see Father Stillmac."

They were both grinning, when Ann Marie came to them and said in a stern, upset voice.

"It's not so damn funny. They broke all of Miss Hester's fine china. They broke her crystal. They stole her silver. They totally decimated the contents of the garage apartment."

Barton put his arm around her and seriously asked, "Who did?"

"Those two renegades that old lady Bydian and that slut, Maudie, hired," hollered Ann Marie.

"How do you know that?" asked the Judge.

"Because Maybelle overheard that witch Bydian telling Maudie Jefferson that she would kick in a 100 dollars if she would get Palomino and Plaster to tear up the place, and give Barton a good whipping. Maybelle called the Chief. He got here too late." She calmed down, looked at Barton, put a very concerned expression on her face, walked right up to him, inspected him from all angles, and started crying.

Barton did not have a scratch on him.

Judge Marbling embraced both of them, started walking toward the house, paused a moment and remarked, "I guess it is time to proceed with the sanity hearings."

Mrs. Marbling walked to the screened portico door, announced that supper was ready.

As they walked from the yard to the screened portico, Barton put his arm around Ann Marie and whispered in her ear, "I love you. And, don't worry, we'll get the apartment fixed in no time."

They sat down to eat. Mrs. Marbling, shaking her head in disgust, said, "I'm so sorry about the apartment."

Ann Marie hugged her mother. "Don't worry anymore, Mama, we'll get it all straightened out in no time."

Judge Marbling chimed, "I forgot to tell you that the Sheriff has recovered the silver. He will get it back to just as soon as possible."

His mind returned to the radio broadcast.

"Where did he find it?" queried Mrs. Marbling.

The Judge looked at Barton with an I'm- not-going-to-tell expression, then answered, "It seems the Sheriff has the culprits. And, unfortunately, Maudie Jefferson committed suicide."

"Committed suicide!" expressed Mrs. Marbling.

"Yes. For whatever reason. Sylvester told me that he saw Mr. Jefferson with his suitcase at the train station. But I don't think that was her reason. It had to be something else."

"Let's eat," Ann Marie said.

The four were almost speechless throughout the meal, and when they had finished they went through the usual dishwashing routine. Ann Marie washed. Barton rinsed. The Judge dried, and Mrs. Marbling returned them to the cabinets. They spoke very little throughout the process.

Barton went to the guest room, knelt to say his prayers and the Rosary, felt the presence of three people he knew who loved him very much. Very little was spoken when the Rosary was over. Judge and Mrs. Marbling left for their bedroom, leaving Ann Marie alone with Barton.

She kissed him on the nose and said, "Get some rest. For

when we are married, I'll keep you up a little later." She flirted out the door to her bedroom.

Judge Marbling arose early and plugged in the coffee pot. He poured a cup, locking the kitchen door behind him. It was 4:30 in the morning.

Paul Bydian met him at the Westside Cafe, where they took a booth.

It had become a custom that when men who normally sit at the long table elect to take a booth, they want a little privacy. This morning, in the booth, Judge Marbling and Paul Bydian wanted to discuss the ramifications of the forthcoming sanity hearing.

"Jarvis has signed a waiver."

"Sara Lou has expressed objections because of what 'they' would say. She has not considered what is best for her grandmother, and we really don't need her consent. I thought, as a courtesy to her, that I would inquire about her feelings on the matter and ask her to attend the hearing," Mr. Paul Bydian said as he moved his coffee cup to permit the breakfast to be served.

"We can convene promptly at 8 o'clock, and begin the proceedings," said the Judge.

Both men finished breakfast, walked across the street, into the square, and up to the second floor where the court room was located. The Probate Judge was already there.

The ambulance parked on the side where the attendants lifted Mrs. Bydian to the ground.

She was still in her wheelchair. They carted the wheelchair up the ramp and into the court house. There was no elevator, nor ramp, so the attendants carried her.

Seated by her father, Sara Lou Bydian did not look at her grandmother as she was being wheeled into the court room. The

attendants placed her between Dr. Beardsley and Mr. Paul
Bydian.

Ole Mrs. Bydian, although seated in the wheelchair, was
propped on her cane. She was staring out the window as if she
was in another world. Her glassy eyes rested above an uneven,
heavy rouged cheek, and her hair gleaned stringy; it hung from
under a yarn tam.

Judge Marbling opened his law book to Title 45, Section
236, and read aloud.

"Mental inferiors and feeble-minded defined. The following
are declared to be mental inferiors or deficients or feeble-minded:

"—All persons of whatever age, who are deficient or inferior
to the extent of being classed in either of the following groups of
the feeble minded.

"—That is to say, idiots, imbeciles, feeble-minded or mo-
rons, and any of whom may be, or may not be epileptics, but not
violent or insane . . . that he is unable to but not violent or insane
. . . that he is unable to manage his affairs with ordinary
prudence, or he is a menace to the happiness or safety of himself
or others in the community, and he requires care, supervision,
and control either for his own protection or for the protection of
others.

"—It is specifically recognized that the greatest danger which
the feeble-minded constitute to the community lies in the
frequency of the passing on of mental defect from one generation
to another . . ."

Upon hearing the Judge read the last paragraph, Sara Lou
jumped up and ran.

She was crying.

Barton, seated in the back row of the court room, got up,
waited for Sara Lou coming up the aisle, stopped her, put his arm

around her shoulder and proceeded with her out of the court room and into the corridor.

He asked her why she was crying, gave her his handkerchief and waited for her explanation.

"I don't know. Maybe it is the condition of grandma, or it may be that I got upset when the Judge read that part passing on the feeble-mindedness from one generation to another, I just don't know." She whimpered as she patted her eyes.

"Sara Lou, we can't run away from our problems."

"I do believe that this problem is one that you will be glad about. We studied, in our Bio-Social course, that little was known about genetics until recently. That law that the Judge read, was probably written in the early twenties, when witchcraft prevailed over science." He spoke convincingly as she handed him his handkerchief.

Ann Marie, left her catechism class at St.Martin's, walked the two blocks to the court house, climbed the stairs, spotted Barton and Sara Lou in the hall, went to them. "And, what are you two beautiful people up to?"

Sara Lou, now smiling, told Ann Marie about being upset and that Barton had consoled her and convinced her that she had not inherited insanity from her grandmother. She put her arm around Ann Marie and stated, "If you decide to discard him, can I have first choice."

Barton answered, "What a nice thing to say. But, now, why don't we attend the rest of the hearing."

The three eased into the court room , sat on the last row of seats and quietly listened to the Probate Judge, now presiding.

"That the person named above is mentally ill and poses a real and present threat of substantial harm to herself and/or to others. That the said danger to herself or to others has been evidenced by recent overt acts, at times and places specified as follows:

"a. She has participated in the deliberate act of hiring hood-lums to ramsack and destroy property of others.

"b. She has repeatedly displayed, in public places, behavior which was so belligerent and shocking to the good conscience of her community that she has been adjudged a nuisance.

"c. By consent of her family, she has not the capacity to understand her actions nor the capability to care for herself nor does she possess the awareness to defend herself.

"d. That she is unreliable and further attempts to help her on an out patient basis would be risky and dangerous.

"That commitment is the least restrictive alternate necessary and available for the treatment of Mary Paulette Bydian's mental illness."

The Probate Judge paused from his reading, peered over his horn rimmed glasses in the direction of Mr. Paul Bydian, and Dr. Beardsley, and asked, "What sayeth the family of Mary Paulette Bydian?"

Mr. Paul Bydian stood, turned around, looked toward the three young people seated in the back row as if to ask Sara Lou her feelings.

Sara Lou stood, gave her father an affirmative nod, then sat down.

Mr. Paul Bydian remarked, "Your honor, the family of Mary Paulette Bydian concur with the findings of the sanity hearing and the results of the commitment proceedings."

The Probate Judge replied, "So be it." He handed the papers to the clerk who came to Mr. Paul Bydian and told him that he would have them ready by mid-afternoon.

Chapter 26

Resident At Brice's

Mary Paulette Bydian remained in a trance throughout the sanity hearing, the commitment proceedings, throughout the night. And into the next day.

The ambulance arrived to take her for the trip to Tuscaloosa.

Her condition had not improved. She displayed no emotion whatsoever when the young ambulance attendant eased her onto the partially elevated stretcher, wheeled her outside, and carefully boarded her into the ambulance and secured the stretcher so that it would not shift en route.

Mr. Paul Bydian's Chevrolet Sedan, with the meager personal effects allowable for residents at Brice, pulled in behind the ambulance. Mr. Paul got out, opened the passenger door for Sara Lou, gave her a reassuring pat on the shoulder, closed the door, walked around, eased into the driver's seat, waved to the ambulance driver to commence the journey, closed his door, cranked the car, put her in gear and proceeded to follow the ambulance.

He kept a safe distance behind the ambulance whose speed was averaging a little over forty miles per hour. He and Sara Lou remained in silence until they reached the Alabama River near Prattville. Sara Lou broke the silence. Glaring over the bridge railings with her wide, sad, remorseful look, she whispered, "I suppose life is like that water down there. It just keeps flowing along. It never stands still."

Mr. Bydian smiled. "Yes. And, at each bend in the river there is forever a changing scene." He paused, gave her a compassionate, fatherly glance, added. "So it is with us today."

After those exchanges of rhetoric, silence ensued once more, with only an occasional recognition of a pretty house, or a pretty garden. When they reached the Cahaba River Bridge at Centerville, Sara Lou raised herself so that she could see the water of the Cahaba, and turned to her father and said, "It ain't standing still, either."

Mr. Paul just grinned and kept following the ambulance ahead.

The ambulance driver stuck his arm out, gave a right turn signal, and drove into the parking lot of a service station.

Mr. Paul did likewise.

The entire party, except Mrs. Paulette Bydian, used the outdoor privies which were modern, by some standards, in that they had running water, and ceramic fixtures in lieu of the usual wooden.

The entourage, once more on the highway, once more in convoy with the ambulance in the lead, and once more moving at forty miles per hour, arrived at Brice Hospital precisely at Two P.M. They had been traveling for five hours since leaving Deer Hill

Mr. Paul went inside.

Very soon, two attendants in white attire, came out, went to the ambulance, assisted the attendants in removing the stretcher which contained Mrs. Paullette Bydian.

They took her into the building, down the hall and into room 128.

Mrs. Paulette Bydian, still in a trance, allowed the attendants to dress her in a gown. They placed her on the other bed in the room, glanced at the lady in the rocking chair, and stated.

"You now have a roommate."

The attendants went into the hallway where Mr. Paul and Sara Lou were waiting, chatted a few seconds about the care that Mrs. Paulette Bydian would receive, turned to walk away, heard a muffling sound coming from room 128, rushed back in, found Mrs. Paulette Bydian lying stretched out on her bed. A pillow over her head. She was dead.

The lady in the rocking chair, staring out the window, rocking feverishly, sang loudly the song "The Spanish Cavalier." She turned her glare from the window toward the attendants, Mr. Paul, and Sara Lou, and with a decretory remark, stated, "Be careful of his birth mark. It seems to be bleeding."

She returned to her singing. The lady in the rocking chair was Aunt Alva.

CHAPTER 27

Judgment Day

The Brice Hospital attendants looked in amazement at the lifeless body perched upon the bed with safety railings up. There was no evidence of any struggle whatsoever. Only the rumpled pillow.

They turned to Mr. Paul Bydian and asked, "What do you make of this?"

Mr. Paul Bydian, his arm around his daughter's shoulder, with an indifferent expression on his face, humbly stated: "I suppose it is her judgment day. May she now rest in peace."

He released the shoulders of his daughter, looking once more at his expired mother. "Sara Lou, let me get in touch with the coroner, maybe we can prevail on McGilvery to wait a couple of hours and transport her back to Deer Hill."

An attendant spoke. "Mr. Bydian, if there is no curiosity on your part, we can sign the death certificate as natural causes, and you can have your people take her now."

"Father, I see nothing which should create any curiosity; and it would be better for us to get her home where she can have an appropriate funeral," Sara Lou said with tears in her eyes.

In spite of all, she loved her grandmother.

"Sign the certificate," spoke Mr. Paul Bydian.

He went out to the McGilvery folks and told them about the

situation. In a matter of minutes, the ambulance, with Mrs. Paulette Bydian on the stretcher-this time in a horizontal position of a corpse-was on its way to Deer Hill.

Mr. Paul and his daughter, once again, were following at a safe distance behind the ambulance. When they got to the Cahaba River, it seemed to be flowing gently at a placid pace.

"Even the waters are calm," Sara Lou said as she stared peacefully at the river.

Mr. Paul Bydian did not respond. He kept driving at the pace of the ambulance. He appeared to be in deep concentration, perhaps recalling the good times with his mother, now departed.

They came to the Alabama River. Mr. Bydian pulled off the highway near Prattville and stopped. He got out and walked a few yards to a position where he could view the water. With Sara Lou at his side, he meditated as the water flowed gently, where before it was with strong splashing currents. He watched the peaceful river for a few more seconds, looked upward to the sky and with an endearing tone, prayed. "Dear God, she is in your hands. Please be patient with her, and above all, grant her peace."

They returned to the car, boarded, started the engine, put her in gear and continued their journey home.

He had lost sight of the ambulance, but he really did not care, for he knew that the funeral home would make the preparations for the interment for tomorrow, the date that he had given the ambulance driver when he left Brice.

Other than his short plea to God on behalf of his mother, Mr. Paul Bydian had been very quiet in his thoughts. When they entered the city limits of Montgomery, he seemed relaxed and asked, "Darling daughter. Are you about hungry?"

Sara Lou gave him a loving smile. "Not just about hungry. I'm hungry."

"Good. Let's stop at the Elite and have a good meal. I think that it will help us to get out of this solemn mood." He remarked, just as he passed the gate to Maxwell Air Force Base.

He drove to downtown near the Elite, but could not find a parking place. He circled the block, went into the below-deck parking of the Exchange Hotel and paid the dollar charge for Elite customers, held the car door open for Sara Lou, took her arm in his, and walked across the street to the Elite. They entered and were met by the maitre'd who promptly escorted them to a small table near the front.

A waiter assisted with the seating and asked about cocktails before dinner.

Mr. Paul Bydian looked toward his daughter as if to ask. She quickly replied to the waiter, "A bottle of Cabernet Sauvignon."

Her father smiled approvingly and winked at her and said in a loving way, "That is exactly what I would have ordered."

Sara Lou returned the smile, then asked, "How do you feel about grandma's fixation about Barton Sandeau?"

"I don't really know. Jarvis was always getting into things which mama thought would be too embarrassing to the family if 'they' found out. So, she spent a lot of time and money covering up his immature behavior."

He grinned. "If papa had been living, he would have taken Jarvis to the woodshed, and in addition, would have made him face up to his misdeeds."

"Do you think that it is possible that Jarvis could be the father of Barton?"

"I truly don't know. It's certainly possible. Jarvis would promise the girls anything. And, I do know because I overheard, that he promised a girl by the name of Alva Sandeau that he would marry her. And, when she became pregnant, mama had a fit.

"She refused vehemently to allow him to marry her. She was so wrought with shame that she sent him to Florida to live with relatives. She lied to the Sandeaus. She told them that he had run away and had joined the French Foreign Legion."

Sara Lou's thoughts drifted from Barton. "At what point does a woman believe a man, particularly when it comes to making love."

"This day and time, I don't know. When your mother and I married, it was traditional for the woman to preserve her virginity until her wedding night. But, today, I do not know." He took a hefty sip of wine and asked, "What are we going to have for dinner?"

"The Trout Amandine."

The waiter took the order, and before the second glass of wine was poured, he returned with the Trout Amandine.

The two ate heartily. Almost in silence. When the meal was finished, so was the wine.

Mr. Paul paid the check and went arm in arm with his daughter. He felt good. It was the first time that the two of them were together that she was treated as an adult.

They drove the one block to US 231, proceeded, slowly, along the way, to their beloved Deer Hill.

At home, they could not get into the driveway, nor at the curb, or anywhere near the house.

The word about Mrs. Paulette Bydian had preceded them. The 'well-wishers' had gathered in campground fashion. They parked their vehicles everywhere including upon the lawn. They had gathered to get the details.

But, details were very limited. She had died of natural causes—that was what had happened.

Mrs. Paul Bydian, however, was in somewhat of a controlled

dither as she had been trying to greet the many "well-wishers," and responding frequently with an "I don't know." She was glad to see her husband who merely answered the queries with, "Natural causes."

Sara Lou was miffed. She could not fathom such a gathering of people who hardly ever spoke to her grandmother, let alone visit her. But, she managed a trumped-up politeness, as she thanked each of them for being so considerate in paying their respects to the family of the late Mrs. Paulette Bydian. She, again, could not fathom why all these people chose to remain in the house just to see who did show up.

It was chaotic.

Sara Lou sensed her mother's waning patience; she went to the phone, called McGilvery's Funeral Home. returned to the parlor, hugged her mother, went to her father and whispered into his ear the conversation she had with McGilverys.

Mr. Paul asked the well-wishers in the crowded parlor if he might have their attention.

Everyone got quiet. Expecting further details. But it was not so.

Mr. Bydian stated that the body was at McGilverys. He invited all to attend the wake, that he and his family would be there in ten minutes.

He went to the door and held it open.

In a very brief time, the once crowded parlor had only three people. Mr. and Mrs. Paul Bydian, and their daughter, Sara Lou.

These three refreshed themselves and went to McGilvery's Funeral Home where Mrs. Mary Paulette Bydian lay in state.

There was not one present who had left the parlor of the Bydian house.

Sara Lou hugged her mother and smiled as she remarked, "I

suppose that their camp meeting ended at the house."

Mrs. Bydian answered, "Thanks for bailing me out. I do not know why people rally around a death. Hardly any of those, who were at the house, ever visited your grandmother, nor, even spoke to her in public. People do funny things."

The wake lasted thirty minutes.

"Jacob. Please close the casket. Seal it for interment."

Mr. Jacob McGilvary shook his hand. Said not a word, watched the three Bydians leave, arm in arm, out of the funeral parlor, headed for home.

The next morning, Mr. and Mrs. Paul Bydian arose, dressed for the funeral services, ate a light breakfast, drove to Oakwood Cemetery for the 9:30 graveside service.

Sara Lou, already dressed in a beautiful organdy dress that seemed to make her glow, radiantly. Had driven her own car to the cemetery, parked in an out of the way space, alighted, paused to view the very small crowd of 'well-wishers' neatly gathered under umbrellas, for fear of more rain, appearing disgruntled that the service of Mrs. Paulette Bydian is being held at this early hour.

As if on cue, Sara Lou began to float across the cemetery grounds in her ankle length, multi- colored dress that seemed to gather air as the skirt stood out as it trailed her movements. Her usually heavy rouged cheeks, a discipline of her dearly departed grandmother, were now much paler; and her smile seemed to accentuate a beauty heretofore not seen in her face. She made her way toward the tent, stopping at the occupied umbrellas, and telling the folks there, "Thank you for coming."

She spotted Ann Marie and Barton standing a short ways behind the interment tent, under a large golf umbrella.

She glided across the freshly mown wet grass path, in her low-heel shoes that were already drenched, but it did not matter, for she appeared an angel suspended from the low hanging, drizzling clouds.

Her every movement was free, far different from other times when she appeared in a crowd and her movements, before, appeared subdued.

Today was different. It was the day of her grandmother's funeral. It was the day that silenced all the chastising from one whom she loved. It was the day that Sara Lou Bydian, in the most indescribable terms, had become free. Free from the eerie constant details of what a young lady should be. Free to decide for herself as to who she was. It was the day that she knew what she was. It was the day that she knew that she was a grown woman; and, her every move reflected such radiant acknowledgment to herself.

She was Sara Lou Bydian—grandaughter of Mrs. Mary Paulette Bydian.

CHAPTER 28

The Library

The eulogy was very brief.

The mourners dispersed.

Mr. and Mrs. Paul Bydian, and their beautiful daughter remained. They had strolled a short distance to await the covering of the grave, and afterwards, returned to place the flowers—especially a pot of golden brown mums with a card of words: "Our deepest sympathy. We love you—We pray for the repose of the soul of your grandmother."

It was signed: Mr. and Mrs. Barton T. Sandeau.

Sara Lou read the card aloud to her parents, hugged them and said, "Ann Marie is one day premature with the signature, but I don't blame her. They truly are two of the most reconciled love birds that I have ever known."

Mrs. Bydian chimed, "I agree."

She added, "I do wish the issue of his parentage could be resolved, and as much as I would love to have him as a nephew, I don't think he deserves the fate of having Jarvis for a father."

Mr. Paul spoke, "My dear darlings. We have just buried one who went to her grave worrying about such matters. And I do believe that we should now put it aside. Maybe in time we will know, and then again, we may never know."

Almost simultaneously the two ladies replied, "Agreed."

Mr. Paul, with a decisive, smirkey sort of a grin concurred and stated, "With his money, I don't believe that the issue of his parentage will be a subject anymore, of our 'do-gooders'."

Mrs. Bydian laughingly replied, "Isn't it amazing what respect a little wealth can bring." She was about to say something else but was hailed by the grave diggers that the grave was now ready for the flowers.

Sara Lou told them that she was going to drop by the Library for a few moments and then she would be on home. She drove out of the cemetery parking area and proceeded to the Library. As she entered the library, she noticed Barton doing some kind of research. He had the log books of the old Orion Female Institute and was carefully examining each page as if he was looking for a specific name.

Barton did not see Sara Lou who had checked out a book, walked over to his table, and whispered, "Thanks for the beautiful pot plant."

Barton raised his eyes, gave her a friendly smile, placed a marker in the log book, took Sara Lou by the arm and walked out into the hall where they could talk without disturbing others.

"How did you like the signature on the pot plant?"

"I liked it. Ann Marie is lucky to get one like you for a husband." She flirted with her eyes as she spoke.

"I'm the lucky one. She is everything that I ever dreamed about." He paused, then said. "And one day, and I do believe one day soon, you will find that Mr. Somebody."

Sara Lou glowed as she responded, "I hope so." She walked down the hall and out of the building.

Barton returned to the log book and eventually found the page which had the name of Jarvis Amos Bydian. Beside his name was an asterisk and a note: "Visiting privileges revoked."

Barton carefully recorded the date of the revocation of Jarvis Bydian's visiting privileges, took from his jacket pocket the two birth certificates, computed 278 days, plus a gestation period of 21 days. The revocation date fell within the parameters computed.

He lingered in this thoughts, then objectively surmised that Jarvis Bydian could have been with Aunt Alva during that time. And if so, he could be the father of himself, or of the baby which was smothered in the hospital.

He scanned, out of curiosity, some of the other names in the log books and noticed several family names of people that he had met during his short stay in Deer Hill. He closed the log book and returned it to the Librarian. While awaiting the return of his sign-out slip, he glanced at a book lying on the counter: *You Can't Go Home Again*, by T. C. Wolf.

He lifted it, glanced at the foreword, then asked himself, "Am I trying to go home again in search of something which appears beyond my reach?"

The librarian returned to him his check-out slip for the log books of the Orion Institute, then asked about the book in his hands, "Would you like to check that one out?"

"Not just yet. I have many other things for the moment to occupy my time, but I would like to read it someday."

He was returning the two birth certificates to his jacket pocket, when Sara Lou came back into the Library and blurted, "Barton, have you a birth mark on your back?"

The Librarian, shocked, put her finger to her lips as a signal to be quiet.

The several people in the library looked up, gawked at Sara Lou, who had committed a brazen act in the sacred sanctuary of books, peered inquisitively at Barton, then returned to their agenda.

Barton grinned, took her by the arm, led her, once again, into the hallway, and inquired, "What was that all about?"

"When my father and I were at Brice's Hospital to enter my grandmother as a patient, we encountered a very strange event. We were waiting in the hallway while the attendants were preparing my grandmother in the clothing of the institution. The attendants came out to visit a moment with us, told us we could go in and visit for a few seconds. We heard this muffling sound. We and the attendants went in and found my grandmother lying stretched on her bed. She had expired." Sara Lou's breathing had now reached a normal pace, so she continued, "The strange thing is that the lady in the room with my grandmother was rocking in a chair and singing verses of "The Spanish Cavalier." She was staring out the window and then turned and glared at us, saying in a very judicial tone, "Be careful. His birth mark is bleeding."

Barton looked concerned. "Please go on," he said.

"I didn't think much about it, not even when daddy told me about Uncle Jarvis dating a young lady by the name of Alva Sandeau, and I didn't think anymore about it until I saw the names on the birth certificates which you had spread out on the table; but, when I got to the car and started to leave, I had this sudden remembrance of that which I have just told you. And, that's when I came into the library to inquire if you had a birth mark."

Barton had not yet understood the connection and he asked Sara Lou, "What does the birth mark have to do with it?"

She placed her hand on his shoulder. "If the lady who made the statement about the bleeding birth mark is, in fact, the lady who smothered her baby in the general hospital, and if she knew that her own baby had such a birth mark, and no one else had

paid any attention to it, then the baby who was smothered—
your cousin—was, in fact, her own baby. And that deduction
makes you the biological son of the parents who raised you."

Barton started crying joyfully, and hugged Sara Lou.

Ann Marie arrived on the scene, and asked, "What is going
on with you two? One crying and one laughing?"

Barton reached out, put his arm around Ann Marie, brought
her into the fold, smiled with small tears seeping down his cheek
and told her that which Sara Lou had just revealed.

The three stood embraced. And in between tears and laughter, Barton kissed each of them on the cheek, released his hold on
them, put his arms into the air, and breathed.

"What a wonderful day this has been."

CHAPTER 29

No Room At The Inn

Ann Marie stepped back from the embrace and remarked, "I almost forgot what it was that I came over here to tell you."

Sara Lou had also stepped back. She asked, "To tell me. Or, this handsome fiancee of yours?"

Ann Marie did not answer her question, instead, she began telling them about Ebb and Flossie.

"I got Flossie on the phone and told her of our plans and asked her if it were possible that she and Ebb could come down this afternoon. She told me that Ebb was not there but that she would get up with him and see about it. Well, she called back and said they they could come and wanted to know if there was a place in Deer Hill where they might stay.

"I called Sylvester at the Inn. He told me in a most apologetic way that they were not permitted to stay at Deer Hill Inn, nor any other hotel in town. And, that he knew of no place where they might be quartered."

Barton flenched. In all his dealings with Ebb and Flossie, there had never been a situation as awkward as this. He asked Ann Marie, "What about Montgomery?"

"Hey, I've got it worked out."

"I went to mama. She and I went to daddy, and it is agreed that they will stay at the garage apartment. And, to make sure that there is no problem about it, Roxy has agreed to stay there also."

She reached up, patted Barton on the head as if he were a little boy, shook her head in disbelief, squinted her eyes, twitched her nose and stated, ""It just doesn't make sense. Ebb, Flossie, Miss Roxy, and others will be welcomed by all who attend the wedding. But, once the wedding is over . . ."

She never got to finish. Sara Lou interrupted and told them that she had to go.

Barton thanked her for her detective work which solved the mystery of his parentage.

He turned to Ann Marie and asked if she wanted to go over to Lanier's Drug and get some of those hot dogs with that special relish.

Ann Marie declined and stated that she had promised to be at the house when Ebb and Flossie arrived, and that should be about three o'clock. She pecked him on the nose and said, "I need to help Roxy get everything ready for this evening. We are having a few guests over after we attend Mass at 5:30."

Barton grinned and helped her get into her Mercedes.

He stood there, watched her drive off, thinking about Ebb and Flossie, knowing full well that he did not want under any circumstances to put them in a compromising position. He was certainly glad that Mrs. Marbling had worked things out. And he did not mind one bit staying one more night at the Deer Hill Inn.

Satisfied that Ebb and Flossie would be all right, he got into his car and drove to Drug Store and Sandwich Shop. As he entered the door, he met Sylvester coming out.

Sylvester, as if making an announcement, said, "I'm looking forward to meeting your servants. I understand that they will be in town to help Miss Roxy with the wedding?" He winked as if to say, "For their benefit."

Barton was not one to deceive, but he trusted Sylvester, so he replied, "Oh. Yes. They should be here this afternoon, and they are scheduled to leave right after the wedding. Ebb has to get back to his job."

There was no doubt that everyone in the sandwich shop had heard Sylvester's announcement. And, for the most part most of them had heard about the deposits that Barton had made. And, none of them appeared troubled that Ebb and Flossie would be helping with the wedding.

Barton either shook hands or waved at the people in the sandwich shop. He sat at one of the stools, ordered two hot dogs with that delicious special sauce, and a cola.

He devoured his lunch, and thought to himself, "Sylvester is a wise man."

CHAPTER 30

Confirmation

Barton left the sandwich shop, walked the three blocks to the Jewelry Store, made a purchase, walked around the square, ran into Mr. Albert, had a short visit about flying, walked back to his car and drove to the airport.

He had been told to make himself scarce for the afternoon, as those at the Marblings had plenty to do to get ready for the party.

Ann Marie was also busy with excitement. She was to be Confirmed at the 5:30 Mass. A party afterwards. And, in the morning, she was to become Mrs. Barton T. Sandeau—a married woman. Her world was moving into another sphere.

She had helped Roxy change the linens on the beds in both bedrooms of the garage apartment. She had helped her mother polish the silver bowls and trays, and she was sweeping the sidewalk when up drove Ebb and Flossie. She dropped her broom, ran to them, embraced them, and told Ebb to put his car in the garage that hers would be used and did not need that space. This, he did.

Ann Marie walked with them to the main house to meet Miss Roxy and Mrs. Marbling.

Roxy was impressed with their manners and their appearance. And, when they asked what can we do. She immediately befriended them and outlined the task that needed to be done.

Flossie immediately pitched in, began to dust the furniture as Ebb came behind and polished it with the lemon oil. Roxy was pleased. Ebb and Flossie were not lazy.

Mrs. Marbling was pleased. Her house was spotless. She gave her approval of the readiness, and invited everyone to the screened portico for a glass of ice tea.

While partaking of the ice tea, Ann Marie revealed to Ebb and Flossie and Roxy that she was to be Confirmed in the Catholic Church at 5:30 and wanted them to attend.

Mrs. Marbling, already privy to that information, again hugged her and said, "What a beautiful thing to do for yourself."

Miss Roxy asked, "Ebb, can you drive us there?"

"It will be my pleasure to be the chauffeur of those so dedicated and hospitable," Ebb answered.

Flossie remarked, "If there is nothing else to do here, let us go to our quarters and prepare ourselves for the confirmation of this beautiful young bride of our Barton."

Roxy, Ebb, and Flossie left the screened portico and walked across the lawn toward the garage apartment. Widow Langur, from her backyard, waved to them. She had been invited to the party. And, now she was a neighbor of friendliness.

A couple of cars passed on the street and the occupants tooted their horns and waved to Roxy, Ebb and Flossie. They must have heard that Barton's two servants had arrived at the Marbling house.

It was almost 4:30, and Ann Marie was beginning to be concerned as to the whereabouts of her beloved Barton when Mr. Albert's car pulled into the drive.

Barton got out bringing with him a string of fish.

Ebb, strolling in the back yard, spotted him, came rushing over, a big grin on his face, hugged Barton, took the string of fish and asked, "My man, where did you get these?"

Mr. Albert got out of the car and shook Ebb's hand. "I thought we would keep him out of trouble. I found him at the airport and we decided to go fishing at a pond. Did we have fun."

Ebb shook his head and replied, "We don't have time to clean them just now as we got to get ready for Mass, then the party. I think that I'll just put them in a tub of water and after the party, you and I can get them cleaned."

Barton smiled at Ebb. "Sounds good to me. But, I don't believe that we will have time. There are over a hundred guests who will be coming and going, and by the time that all of them have left, and by the time we have cleaned the dishes, and the house; we will not feel like scaling these fish. I thought that I would take them over to Roxy's house and give them to her folks."

"That's a good idea," replied Ebb.

Barton shook Mr. Albert's hand. "Many thanks for a wonderful afternoon. I truly enjoyed the fishing." Then he added, "We'll see you, and Miss Annie at the party."

Mr. Albert got back into his car and drove off.

Ebb took the fish to the garage where Miss Roxy already had a wash tub under the spigot. She had overheard Barton tell Ebb that he was giving the fish to her folks, so she wanted to make sure that they did not spoil. She told Ebb. "Macon, my man, is coming by in few minutes. He'll get the fish."

Before she could fill the wash tub, Macon drove up in his pickup. Miss Roxy waived to him, held up the string of fish. "Macon, look what that Barton has done caught, and he wants us to take them to our house and enjoy them."

Macon came over, took the fish, put them on some paper, and left for the ice house. He returned, grabbed a broom, put the finishing touches to the sidewalk where Ann Marie had been working when Ebb and Flossie arrived.

All others were getting dressed for the Confirmation and Mass at St. Martin's Catholic Church.

Flossie, satisfied with her attire, brought out a case and opened it in front of Miss Roxy. "Miss Hester, his mother, gave these to me to save for his wife, and to give them to her on the eve of her wedding. Would you like to give these to Ann Marie?"

Miss Roxy answered, "If you want me too. I love that child just like you love that Barton."

Flossie glanced once more into the mirror, smoothed her dress, left with Roxy and Ebb for the main house to see if they could assist there. But there, everyone was also dressed and sitting in the parlor.

Miss Roxy walked straight to Ann Marie, opened the case, brought forth a strand of cultured pearls.

"I never met Miss Hester, but I knows she was always thinking about her Barton; and, she must have been thinking about you even though she never met you. She wants you to have these as a gift from her and Mr. Mathew."

Crying, Ann Marie went into Roxy's arms, turned around with her makeup slightly in disarray, and gave a gasp of excitement. "Miss Roxy, no one could have said that any better. I wish she could be with us now. I know she is with us in spirit. So is Mr. Matthew." She paused to regain her composure. "Through Ebb, Flossie and Barton, I do feel like I know Miss Hester and Mr. Mathew, and I cherish this gift." She put the pearls around her neck, peered into the mirror, and asked, "Give me a moment to straighten my make up and we'll get over to the church and receive another gift."

Judge and Mrs. Marbling took Ann Marie with them. Ebb

drove Miss Roxy and Flossie. Barton followed and stayed with them until they were seated in the church.

A few guests were present at the Mass, some Catholics, and others, friends of the Marblings.

Father Stillmac proceeded with the Mass, and then followed with the Confirmation ceremony for Ann Marie, and for Julia. After the Sacrament of Confirmation, Communion Rites were presented to the Catholics present. Ann Marie, with an accomplished looking smile, turned to Barton and said, "I did it for myself."

Barton understood, approached her in the presence of several of those who were congratulating her, took from his pocket, another case, opened it, and put around her neck a Diamond Cross. Then with his nose ever so close to hers he whispered, "Congratulations. I love you."

Flossie and Miss Roxy left the church with Ebb, their chauffeur, returned to the house ahead of the Marblings and began preparing the trays to place on the several immaculately, yet conservatively, decorated tables.

In a short time, Judge and Mrs. Marbling returned, followed by Ann Marie and Barton, and soon thereafter, the guests. In all, about a hundred guests came. And in almost every case, Ebb, Flossie, and Miss Roxy made an impression.

Center stage was Ann Marie displaying her pearls and admiringly telling that they were a gift from Barton's parents. And then she displayed her diamond necklace, swooned, and stated, "This is from my beloved."

And when all the guests had departed, seven tired people set about cleaning the dishes,and getting the house in order. For tomorrow, the wedding. And, shortly thereafter, Ebb and Flossie would return home. The Marblings and the Sandeaus would depart for Cuba. Miss Roxy would be left in charge of the house.

Ebb put his arm around Barton and sincerely stated: "I'm sure glad we don't have to clean those fish."

CHAPTER 31

The Night Before

Barton kissed Ann Marie good night, went to his car, drove to the Deer Hill Inn, procured a room for the night—his last night of being alone— took the key from the night clerk, climbed the stairs to the second floor, and went into his room.

He removed his jacket and was about to undress when a knock came upon the door.

He opened it. There stood Sylvester with a silver tray, a bottle of champagne, and two ornate glasses.

Barton grinned, beckoned his friend to enter. "Entré Nous, Monsieur," a remnant from his high school French. "Oui, Monsieur," replied Sylvester. They both laughed."Are we ever bilingual!"

Sylvester entered, placed the tray on a table. "My young friend. I will not be able to attend your wedding tomorrow, so I thought that I would have a night cap with you; and it seems appropriate that it be a bottle of champagne, on this tray, with these two glasses, as the last time I brought them to you, they were not used."

Barton hugged Sylvester, spoke softly, "My dear friend, they were used . . . they were used to hold messages that brought me the most adorable girl in the world."

He hesitated, then continued, "And, they brought me you, a

dear and trusted friend." He walked to the table, lifted the bottle of champagne, and asked, "Sir, shall I pour?"

Ann Marie, bedecked in her pearls, her diamond necklace, her diamond ring, and the big amethyst on her right hand, sat in her father's lap with her arms around his neck, asked, "How did you feel the night before you and mama married?"

Judge Marbling stroked her hair, looked lovingly at his wife, and answered, "I wanted to be with your mother, but tradition prevailed, I had to go home. My father came into my room carrying a small flask of scotch and two glasses. He told me that my mother would have a fit if she saw him giving me a drink of scotch, but he thought it to be appropriate.

"But to his surprise, and mine, my mother came in carrying a glass and remarked, 'You two are not going to leave me out. If I am going to give my son to that beautiful girl, then I'm going to do it in style.' She gulped the small amount of scotch and retreated to her room."

Mrs. Marbling came over and sat on the Judge's other knee, inquired, "You never told me that."

The Judge laughed and retorted. "I didn't want you to know that my mother drank."

Roaring with a slight bluster of laughter, Ann Marie got off the Judge's knee, "That is about as cute as it can get. Let's toast to that, with a crème de menthe."

She went to the dry bar and fetched the drinks.

Ebb was holding Flossie in his arms. "I am awful glad that we came down. I wanted to for Miss Hester, Mr. Mathew. I wanted to for Barton. I wanted to for Miss Ann Marie. And, I wanted to for me and you."

Flossie rolled over and kissed him good night. "Me, too," she said, then felt his muscle and continued.

Macon had gone to his house to check the ice on the fish and returned to the Marblings to wait for Roxy.

On the way home, Roxy smiled at him. "You know honey, that Ann Marie sure knew what she wanted, and she sure knew how to get it. That Barton loves her." Then she winked and added."And, I sure knew what I wanted. And, I sure did get him."

Macon smiled, looked possessively at Roxy. "And, you sure knew how to get him." They both chuckled. He drove the pickup into a small, hidden, thicket. Got out, walked around, opened the door, took her by the hand and walked a short distance.

Sara Lou had left the Marbling's party on the arm of Robert Maxwell, a football player for the University of Alabama, who was visiting his roommate, who arranged the date.

Robert Maxwell: not a large person, six feet, one hundred eighty pounds, dark hair, olive skin, blue eyes, well mannered, neatly attired, and shy. He arrived at the Bydian's home in a pick up truck furnished by his roommate. He parked at the curb, walked to the door, knocked. The door opened. He was greeted by Mr. Paul Bydian who shook his hand, asked him to come in, that Sara Lou would be in shortly.

Mrs. Bydian entered, silently swooned at his good looks, shook his hand, spoke, "Welcome. It is a pleasure to meet you. I understand that we will see you at the Marbling's party."

Sara Lou entered, and slightly, silently, swooned. Flirting her eyes, she thought, "What a handsome 'blind-date'."

She glanced at her mother who gave her that female twitch. "I certainly approve."

Sara Lou returned the glance, spoke quietly, "We may be a little late getting in. We have been invited to a jam session at the college."

On the curb, at the pick up truck, Sara Lou, somehow got some grease on her dress and returned to the house to change. She met her parents leaving for the party, held apart the area of the grease, to show her mother the predicament. Without stopping to explain, she continued into the house in search of something else to wear.

Robert Maxwell wiped the grease spot off the pick-up truck, returned to the house to clean his hands. He located the bathroom between the two rear bedrooms. It had three doors. One from the hall. And one into each bedroom. He opened the hall door and walked in. The door to Sara Lou's bedroom was open. He glanced. She was naked, browsing in her closet.

She heard his footsteps, turned, he was standing in the door. For whatever reason, she remembered Mary Louise's words: "You will know." She knew.

They were late for the party.

At the house where the Bydians were still up, Robert and Sara Lou came into the parlor. She flashed the championship ring (Rose Bowl 1946), on her third finger, left hand, for her parents to see.

Calmly, sweetly, radiantly beautiful, (and no longer a virgin), she told her parents, "We're engaged."

Robert was beaming, his clothes a bit rumpled.

The Bydians embraced him. Congratulated him. "We Certainly approve." They excused themselves, leaving the two betrothed to themselves.

Robert's clothes became more rumpled.

Sara Lou walked out on the porch with him, kissed him, told him that she would see him next weekend for his fraternity party. She waved as he drove away.

She went into the house and out to the kitchen where her parents were having a slight repast. They arose, hugged her, still elated for her, held her hand up to view, once more, the Championship Ring.

She twirled it with her right hand, looked shyly to her parents and announced., "My dearest parents. I am no longer a traditionalist. I am in love."

They understood.

CHAPTER 32

The Wedding

Barton and his best man, Mr. Albert Rose, stood in the cry room awaiting the signal to approach the altar.

Mrs. Paul Bydian, an accomplished organist, was playing the huge pipe organs.

Ann Marie, dressed in a pale green, two piece suit with a ruffled blouse, a small brim hat with a matching ribbon, and minimal cosmetics—not necessarily needed as the natural glow of her skin accentuated every facial feature down to the slight dimple in her chin—waited in the vestibule with her mother, and her bridesmaid, the radiantly beautiful, Sara Lou Bydian. They were nervous and happy.

Father Stillmac concluded the abbreviated Mass, walked to the Altar, faced the congregation of friends and relatives, signaled Mrs. Paul Bydian who began playing the wedding march, "Here Comes The Bride."

Barton and Mr. Albert walked to the altar.

Ann Marie and Sara Lou walked to the altar.

"Let us pray," Father Stillmac said to the congregation.

At the conclusion of the prayer, congregation still standing, Father Stillmac asked, "Who giveth this woman to be the bride of Barton T. Sandeau?"

Judge Marbling replied, "Her mother and I do."

He moved beside Mrs. Marbling, and the entire congregation sat down.

The wedding ceremony took all of fifteen minutes. Father Stillmac announced, "I now pronounce you man and wife."

The bride sighed. "At last."

CHAPTER 33

Cuba Bound

The newlyweds left the church premises riding in the the 1933 Plymouth, with but one small ribbon attached to the self installed radio antenna; put there by Ebb as his token of love; drove directly to the Marbling home, went to the front door, cracked it open. Barton picked her up , carried her through the threshold, embraced her with a very passionate kiss; thinking they were alone, feeling amorous, yet knowing that their pre marital's would have to suffice as Ann Marie needed, at least, one more day for her menstrual cycle.

The applause assured him that they were not alone. There stood, Mr. and Mrs. Marbling, Ebb, Flossie, Macon and Miss Roxy, and Mrs. Hecht, her grandmother from Oberammergau, Germany. She had arrived just in time to get to the church for the wedding.

Mrs. Hecht had observed the 1933 Plymouth as it came into the drive. She took her turn to hug and congratulate Ann Marie and in doing so whispered."Why don't I give you a new car for a wedding present?"

Ann Marie returned the hug, and the whisper, "I expect that I need to discuss that with my husband. And, I am most certain that he will think that to be an excessive gift."

She hugged her grandmother once more and asked, "What

are you going to do while we are on our honeymoon?"

"Oh! Mary Margaret has told me that she and the Judge are going with you to Cuba, so I have planned a tour of the western part of the United States."

Mrs. Marbling came to her mother and remarked, "We are getting ready to leave. Miss Roxy will assist you while we are gone; and, we hope you have an excellent tour."

At 11;15, Barton and Ann Marie arrived at the airport, signed the papers for Mrs. Wards, took the over-water gear, went out to the Stinson, placed it in the conveniently designated places, returned for their allocated two soft clothing bags; one makeup kit, and one shaving kit, took them to the Stinson, arranged them in the rear baggage compartment, leaving that door open awaiting the Marbling's baggage.

Ann Marie went to the car, fetched the picnic basket, locked the car, left the keys with Mrs. Wards, returned to the Stinson, placed the picnic basket in the small luggage area behind the high-back stuffed couch, where it would be easily accessible when the wide, double arm rest, is in the down position.

Barton had filed an IFR Flight Plan which included penetrating the ADIZ over the Gulf of Mexico to St Petersburg, Florida, their first intended comfort and refueling stop.

The Marblings arrived at 11:45. They came around the hangar carrying their baggage and a waving as if to say, "Don't leave us."

Ann Marie met them, took Mrs. Marbling's soft clothing bag, placed it in the rear baggage compartment, took the Judge's and placed it, followed by the makeup kit, and the shaving kit. She closed, and latched the rear baggage compartment.

Precisely at 12 o'clock the Stinson lifted off the runway at Deer Hill, climbed to 2,000, received her IFR clearance, climbed on course to 7,000 feet where she leveled off, and engaged the auto pilot.

The navigators, now a threesome, reported true airspeed—145 miles per hour.

The navigators, with the sectionals clearly charted, recognized Marianna to the west, then Panama City, then at a distance of about twenty five miles, they viewed the west coast of the pennisula—Florida. They were over the waters of the Gulf of Mexico.

"What is that town over there?" asked Ann Marie.

"Perry, Florida." Answered the Judge who had been tracking the route on the sectional chart given to him by Barton before they departed Deer Hill.

The entire west coast of the Gulf of Mexico was never out of sight even though Barton had flown through the ADIZ and was, in fact, outside the continental limits of the United States.

Two hours and fifteen minutes, the Stinson sat smoothly down at St. Petersburg.

The comfort stop was welcomed. The refueling was necessary. And, thirty minutes later the Stinson, with its eager crew and passengers, was on its way to Miami.

At 5:45 EST, she was on her approach, over the Everglades, at an altitude of 1,000 feet, trimmed for the landing. In minutes, the Stinson was on the ramp at Tamiami Airport.

Barton secured the plane, took from the rear baggage compartment the chosen soft bag for each couple who had packed together the clothes for the stop in Miami. Shaving kits and makeup kits were removed, and the door was again locked. The picnic basket now diminished to the non perishables was left in the plane.

The honeymooners took a cab to the Mc Alister Hotel near

Biscayne Boulevard, registered for their rooms, adjacent to each other, caught the elevator to the fifth floor, agreed to have dinner at Joe's Stone Crab House at eight o'clock, sat their gear down and unlocked the door.

Barton lifted Ann Marie, and this time officially carried her over the threshold.

Judge Marbling, noticing with pleasure, picked up his wife and carried her over the threshold.

They would have about an hour and a half before departing for dinner.

Mrs. Marbling tapped on the door to the room of Barton and Ann Marie and announced, "We should be leaving in about twenty minutes."

Ann Marie, looking chic in her newly acquired organdy, knee length, low cut—back and front—dress, and her pearls, eased her mother back into the hall and hugged her affectionately.

"I don't know what I would have done if you had not given me your secret. It worked wonderfully." She smiled, "We could possibly have started our family."

She embraced her mother again and asked, "Hope you had as much fun as we did."

Mrs. Marbling responded as she fluffed her hair. "You can bet on that."

They were both giggling when the Judge and Barton joined them in the hall.

"I've asked the Bell Captain to call us a cab." Then in the next breath, "What are you two giggling about." The Judge asked as he shook his head and led them to the elevators.

They entered the lobby where the bell captain promptly pointed to the cab alongside the curb in front of the Hotel. The Judge tipped the bell captain, then the four made their way to the cab which took them to Joe's Stone Crab House.

They ate stone crabs and drank Chablis until they were completely satisfied. The Judge paid the fare and remarked pleasantly, "A partial payment on an expensive wedding gown that we did not have to purchase."

They caught the cab back to the Mc Alister, went into the Bar, and at the Judge's suggestion, ordered a crème de menthe, creating quite a stir when they told the bartender that one couple, on their honeymoon, were the parents, chaperoning the other couple who were on their honeymoon. The Bartender was in awe. No one bothered to explain.

Early Sunday morning, Barton checked the weather.

He went back to the bed and to Ann Marie. After the loving, he told her that the weather was predicted to be beautiful all day, and all over the Caribbean. It should be a great day for flying.

Ann Marie called her parent's room to tell them. When her mother answered, she asked, "Am, I interrupting anything?"

Mrs. Marbling teased, "You're a little late for that."

Ann Marie reported about the beautiful weather in store for the day.

With baggage in hand, the four left the Mc Alister, boarded a cab which took them to Tamiami Airport.

Judge and Mrs. Marbling went inside and paid the account. He winked, "Another installment."

She laughed, "It is going to be the prettiest dress that has ever been made."

Barton completed the pre flight, filed his IFR to Key West, returned to the Stinson, again checked all visible components, helped his passengers into the plane, and at 9:30, 483 Alpha George was in the air enroute to Key West. At 10:45, she was on final approach to the Key West Airport.

They deplaned, went to the operations office, filed the manifest to fly to Havana; and filed the permit to take a US Registered Airplane into a foreign country.

In thirty minutes they were airborne, with a full tank of gas, adequate for a round trip flight and some reserve; also on board was a gourmet lunch of conch fritters and lemonade, acquired by Mrs. Marbling and Ann Marie.

Once level at 4,000 feet, and on course with trim tabs adjusted for the wind, Barton again refreshed his passengers in the use of the over water gear and he emphasized, "In all cases, remain calm and in control."

The 90-mile flight to Havana, Cuba took exactly 40 minutes from take off to touchdown.

At the Havana Airport, the attendant asked in Spanish. "Asesinar usted quiere poner a la percha la aeroplane. Esta' alli mucho ma's seguro."

Ann Marie laughed. "I think he wants to know if you want to put the plane in the hanger. It will be much safer there."

The attendant said, "Si." Then in perfect English he asked Barton if he wanted to hanger the Stinson. He quickly added, "It will be much safer there."

Barton chose the hanger, gave the attendant the service order, told him the approximate date of departure, unloaded the baggage—leaving the empty picnic basket—and made his way into operations where he presented the manifest and the permit, and paid the fifty cents per person tax assessed for the paper work.

Once cleared, they caught a cab to the Plaza Hotel.

CHAPTER 34

A Love Affair

The Tour, THE SUMMER LAND OF THE WORLD, took them to the Prado, the Presidential Palace, the LaFuerza Fortress, the La Punta, the Centro Gallego, Morro Castle, Columbus Cathedral, and many other points of interest.

On a plateau, over looking Guantanomo Bay, they lunched in a very quaint, thatched cafe. Ann Marie tried her Spanish. She wrote it down before she spoke to the waiter. Senor Podamos los tacos han refrito las judias guacomole ensalada y cerveza?

Mrs. Marbling surprised everyone. She remarked, "I have not had tacos, refried beans, or guacomole salad in a long time. The beer will be welcomed, too."

"Si," the Judge replied laughing.

The Tour continued for another two hours before returning to the Plaza.

In the lobby of the Plaza Hotel, Judge Marbling suggested, "Let's get some refreshments before we go up."

In the Grill of the Plaza, they ordered Daiquiris. "What time do we want to meet for dinner?" Mrs. Marbling asked.

"In about two hours," answered Ann Marie as she eyed her beloved husband.

"Sounds great," echoed Judge Marbling as he eyed his beloved wife.

"Hope that's enough time," echoed Barton as he left eagerly with Ann Marie and headed for the elevator. They were followed by Judge and Mrs. Marbling.

After the loving, Mrs. Marbling, cuddled in the arms of the Judge, asked, "Henry, what do you think of our Son?"

"I am proud of him and Ann Marie. They have brought a new meaning into our lives. And, if we are blessed with grandchildren, and it appears that is a possibility, our lives will be further enriched. Their young love is like a gale that brings fresh cleansing air. I love them very much. And, yes, they are truly A FRESH GALE."

About the Author

William Sanford, born in Bessemer, Alabama, graduated from Hueytown High School, before receiving a bachelor of Science Degree from Troy State University. He earned a Masters of Education Degree from Auburn University before going on to study law at Jones Law University. He served in the U.S. Navy during World War II as a radioman, and a radio teletype operator. He holds a Private Pilots License, airplane single and multi-engine land, instrument rated airplane.

Married for over fifty years to Cornelia Kreis of Troy, Alabama, he has five children and eleven grandchildren.

He has three other books to be published: *The Price of Cotton*, *Tainted Quill*, and *Their Story*. This is his first book.